A COLD CONSPIRACY

Preface

In June 1999, after a gap of almost three hundred years, Scotland, once again, gained its own Parliament. While she remains part of the United Kingdom, it has meant, inevitably, that the Scottish Government is increasingly looking at its own international relationships without necessarily going through the Foreign Office in London. When this book, under its original title, *Norslag* (published in the United States as *Folio Forty One*), was first published way back in 1972, the idea of Scotland having its own Parliament was still a distant prospect. Yet the concept of having a semi-conspiratorial group of dissident nationalists bent on closely uniting Scotland with its Scandinavian neighbours was not so far fetched. For many centuries, after all, large parts of Scotland were owned by Norway, and the relationship between Scotland and the Baltic States remained an extremely strong one throughout many hundreds of years.

"Folio Forty One" is the secret British Government file on a group called "the Norsemen". Whether they are dedicated to the overthrow of the British Government or to building a Northern European Federation of States is at first far from clear, and Whitehall's imperative is to find out what is really going on. As would probably happen even today, a young Scotsman is charged with finding out. The consequent conflict between his personal loyalties and his public duties arises especially when he rekindles a past love affair with a girl who is part of the central directorate of the Norsemen themselves.

If I were asked to revise this book, I would make few changes. It has stood the test of time. Things are never as they seem, and in the world of international intrigue, even today, for every spy or traitor dramatically uncovered, a hundred remain. In the cold waters that flow between Scotland and Scandinavia, there are no real icebergs, but the metaphor holds good: when you see one, only the tip shows and the real magnitude of its threat lies hidden beneath the grey waves.

Michael Shea, October 2000

A COLD CONSPIRACY

Michael Shea

Severn House

This title first published in Great Britain 2000 by
SEVERN HOUSE PUBLISHERS LTD of
9–15 High Street, Sutton, Surrey SM1 1DF.
Originally published 1972 as *Norslag,*
under the pseudonym *Michael Sinclair.*
This title first published in the USA 2001 by
SEVERN HOUSE PUBLISHERS INC of
595 Madison Avenue, New York, N.Y. 10022.

British Library Cataloguing in Publication Data

Shea, Michael, 1938-
A cold conspiracy
1. Strategic alliances (Business) - Europe, Northern - Fiction
2. Suspense fiction
I. Title
823.9'14 [F]

ISBN 0-7278-5620-0

To M. G. S. and K. S.

Printed and bound in Great Britain by
MPG Books Ltd, Bodmin, Cornwall.

ONE

Oslo, Friday Evening

Drammensveien . . . 11.15 p.m. to be precise. The day had been warm for late February but the night temperature had dropped to seven degrees below and a thickening crust of ice had formed over the slush on the pavements. The months of the clean white Norwegian winter were now almost gone and ahead lay the dismal, ugly weeks of the slow thaw into a spring that would suddenly emerge towards the end of April. The snow had left the pine trees and the rooftops and lay blackening in the city grime. The road surfaces, at last scraped more or less clear, were potholed and broken by their long burial in the extreme cold.

Tinker—he had been among friends that evening—stumbled and slipped his way between the piles of dirty ice and snow heaped by the roadside. He passed a group of well-clad road-men working in the lamplight with mechanical digger and lorry, carting away these frozen heaps of winter, to dump them like refuse in the black waters of the fjord.

Sod the Norwegian Blue Laws. The further north one went in Europe, the shorter the licensing hours. Calvinism—a reason or an excuse—was more rampant than in Scotland. They had just started on the hard stuff. As if the confounded climate wasn't enough.

A boisterous, laughing group of young people pushed past Tinker, going in the other direction. They too had obviously just been expelled from some bar, but, unlike him, they were fortified and supplied for their private party to come. He heard the clink and saw the sparkle of lamplight on bottles as they made their noisy way on down the street.

He turned enviously to watch them but as he did so, lost his footing, crashed against a parked car, and slid almost gracefully on to the snow. Contact with the cold brought him sufficiently to his senses for him to struggle to his feet again. An hour's drunken sleep in the snow meant frostbite if not worse.

Over by the fjord, the floodlighting still shone on the three masts and countless ropes of the great training ship, the *Christian Radich.* Against the clear night sky, the rigging stood in delicate contrast to the heavy office blocks along the waterfront. A car drove quickly past, tyres breaking through the coating of ice and sending a shower of blackened slush over Tinker. He shouted an English curse after it and was still shouting when the policeman came up to him. The officer was sympathetic. He had every right to be angry, but it didn't do to disturb the peace of the Oslo night. Could he get him a taxi?

But Tinker wanted to walk. It would clear his head. He had been celebrating, celebrating Norwegian independence with some friends, he added as an afterthought.

The policeman remarked that it was still three months till the National Day. Stifling a hiccup, Tinker replied gravely that one had to celebrate when one could. Who could say where he would be on the seventeenth of May. The policeman smiled understandingly and went on his way with a last word of caution for the Englishman.

Two hundred metres and three falls later, Tinker decided the policeman had been right. He would summon a taxi. He drew a battered pink copy of the *Financial Times* from his overcoat pocket. He would wave it. Then any passing taxi would be sure to notice.

He steadied himself drunkenly against a doorway, preparing to wait. Above his head, the light from a street lamp caught the polish on the big brass plate beside the door that announced the Embassy. . . .

A car was coming. . . . Certain to be a taxi at this time of night. He stepped forward, waving his paper. But the car wasn't going to stop. It was travelling too fast. He pulled back urgently to cover himself from the expected spray of filthy slush and just at that moment the grenade hit him.

TWO

Edinburgh, Sunday Evening

The plane had been delayed and it was nearly midnight. The Minister settled back in his reserved First Class seat by a window and discreetly loosened his shoe laces. Then he stretched out contentedly, feet deep under the wide space beneath the seat in front, glad yet again that the days of cramped legs in tourist accommodation were over for ever. A major benefit of rank was the comfort which the taxpayers' money so gratefully provided. The Minister formulated this thought more for simple self-amusement rather than out of any deep-rooted cynicism. He yawned.

Nodding briefly to a fellow M.P., he deliberately looked down and started fumbling with his brief case. He didn't want company on the journey. He had work to do. That was the trouble with this flight. When the House was in session, all the Scottish M.P.s from the east coast were on it after weekending in their constituencies. He should take the overnight train and get a good night's sleep.

The flight was fully booked and a man took the seat beside him. Thank God, not one of his colleagues. The face was unfamiliar but the Minister gave him an automatic electioneering smile just to be on the safe side, and then settled down to his papers.

As he did so, he caught a momentary glimpse of his reflection in the plane window. The slightly heavy features, the undisciplined, prematurely greying hair and the inevitable bow-tie which, to his delight, the political cartoonists were beginning to notice, when they noticed him at all.

He tested a slight and discreet smile on his reflection. It still looked convincing enough: warm, capable, reassuring. In a moment of truth his election agent had once told him that it was his most valuable political asset. *One* of his most valuable political assets, the man had quickly corrected himself. The local polls confirmed that it certainly brought home the women's votes. The Minister had never known whether to be flattered by the remark, but he had employed his smile liberally ever since. Why not? If his popular public image was a warm and attractive one, did it so much matter if, on closer acquaintance, the smile appeared a little less genuine, a little more contrived? Did it matter that an opponent had once dubbed him the "smiler with the knife". The nickname was almost attractive in itself and he had used it in his campaign to attack that same opponent. "Charity, yes. Warmth, yes. But as my record shows, I have never been afraid to pick up the knife when it comes to cutting away inefficiency and waste." The Minister had written that part of his speech himself and it had gone down well. He smiled again at the memory and his reflection in the window smiled back. He looked away self-consciously for fear that someone might have noticed.

"Captain Trugood and his crew welcome you on board this BEA Vanguard flight to Heathrow. We must apologise for the slight delay, which was caused . . ." The loudspeaker system crackled and the voice became barely audible above the roar as the engines revved up for take-off.

The Minister half-heartedly shuffled through his folder of briefs. He was tired. He should have brought his Private Secretary with him. Philip could at least have sorted out some of the letters while he himself was making that party speech at Lochinver, though he always felt it was a bit hard taking that boy away from his Kent weekend with his wife. *Boy*. He almost laughed. At thirty-five, Philip was only three years younger than himself. Rank made one forget sometimes, and that was a dangerous trend.

"Something to drink, Minister?" The slightly over made-up stewardess recognised him.

"No, I have work . . . oh, why not. Bring me a whisky please. Support home industries," he joked feebly.

He put his papers away and locked his briefcase. He would

get up early tomorrow instead. Enough was enough. All day Saturday with electioneering, speeches, ringing doorbells, shaking hands. It was a hopeless case anyway and the Nationalists were bound to get in at the Lochinver by-election. Then today, hours spent listening to the ragbag of constituents' grievances. Least of all he liked the time he had to spend at his political "surgery"; a necessary but debasing part of his work. The vast majority of it was of a nature that made him feel more like a family doctor than a politician. Or a sanitary inspector. This weekend, for example, he had had a spate of faulty drainage complaints. He had listened attentively, forcing sympathy out of a growing irritation and then had passed his grateful constituents into the proper hands of their local town councils. This was not the stuff of politics. It might be a role for some of his lesser colleagues. It was not and never would be his, especially so now that he was a junior Minister. His political agent would have to do more in future. He was paid enough. Besides, it left him only a few moments of peace with his wife and the baby. At times he could almost pack it in. With his background, his personality, T.V. would take him back like a shot. But inevitably, his political ambitions barred that exit.

He picked up a bundle of unread weekend papers, symbols of his lack of leisure. The *Scotsman* and the *Observer* were both predicting a Nationalist win at the Lochinver by-election. It was a safe bet. Then there was more Middle East trouble. Why couldn't they fight it out in their own back yard? It was big enough. No, they had to involve everyone. Now there had been a new bomb attack at one of the embassies in Oslo which couldn't be more remote from the scene. That was all embassies were for these days. Attacks used to be confined to U.S. Information Offices. Saturday's *Scotsman* carried a full report and the *Observer,* with a later Oslo dateline, followed the story up with the news that a man, an English businessman, had been killed. Some policeman had spoken with the innocent victim just before it had happened.

"Your drink, Minister."

He took the whisky with some ice and a very little water, and turned thankfully to the book reviews.

Whitehall, Monday Afternoon

"All very curious," Rossetti was saying. "The Ambassador of Suspect Country Number One was summoned at twelve—you know who I mean. We had checked with Oslo first, of course, to see that they didn't mind us taking it up separately. The Foreign Secretary was all lined up to give him a fair hammering, and then, perky as anything, His Excellency turns round and says his country had absolutely nothing to do with it. Too cold in the snow for their freedom fighters or something. He's not usually modest about these things, so I'm afraid we'll have to believe him."

His fellow civil servant audience looked somewhat bored, but Rossetti had been dragged early from his bed that morning and wasn't going to give in so easily. He was the Ministry's Civil Servant dealing with acts of terrorism and associated matters. How he had come to such a potentially important desk was the subject of much indignant office gossip, since his intellectual ability was not widely regarded as being great, though few questioned his role as a latter-day Beau Brummel, nor queried the impeccability of his background. Rossetti always appeared rather out of place in the modern Civil Service, a latter-day fop in the dull world of green painted walls, grey steel desks and tea urns. To many of his more mundane colleagues, his studied dilettantism was an insulting intrusion into the intricate machinery of Government, and yet somehow he continued to survive and prosper like a pet peacock in a factory farm.

"My brief wasn't even used," he went on. "Hours spent on it! 'Infringement of national rights and question of trespass nothing to do with H.M.G., but killing of a British subject very much our concern.'—That was the line. You know the sort of thing. And not even used. . . ." Rossetti stood up and stared petulantly around the dreary green office. He appeared to take the whole thing as a personal insult.

An elderly woman in a dirty white smock who was pushing a tea trolley, bashed her way into the room and interrupted his monologue. By the marks on the heavy brown door, one could see she had been doing it for years.

"... 'ow many wiv milk?" she demanded. Dutiful hands shot up. "Don't ferget termorrer's tea-money day." She gave a threatening look to remind everyone as she splashed the four chipped cups down on a table by the door. There were numerous further bangs and she disappeared on her afternoon round.

"I'm going early, that's all I can say." Rossetti paced irritably across the cracked linoleum and picked up a cup. "Eight o'clock this morning. Would you believe it? Reminds me of the Suez Crisis . . . God!" he exclaimed. "Now look at that. . . . That bloody tea woman's poured it all in the saucer again."

Argyllshire, Tuesday Morning

Gently . . . gently. Slow. . . . There it was. The line ran out fast and then went taut. He watched the ripples spread out across the water. Slack, and he wound in quickly. The fish came in to only a few yards from him, arching and straining desperately in the shallow pools among the rocks. He wound again, locked the reel and picked up the net. A splash or two, a short struggle and it was all over for the salmon.

Calder MacCaig had hardly noticed the rain before. Now he could feel it running down his neck. That was enough. The catch had been well worth the early rise. He clambered over the treacherously smooth rocks, away from the river and then began to walk slowly up the hill, waders folded down from his thighs. Now it was raining hard but he liked that sort of weather, not just for the fishing. It freshened him and made him feel properly fit once again.

The cloud hung low over the hills by the firth and the high mountains behind were completely obscured. The bracken ran from the footpath in an unbroken belt across the moor towards the Forestry Commission plantation of young firs which in its turn disappeared in the mist. A bleak and inhospitable scene to anyone unfamiliar with Argyllshire at that season of the year, but to him it was agreeable in its very solitude. He could almost be happy to spend a lifetime in such surroundings, except that he knew deep inside himself, that such an existence would send him to mental sleep within a year.

As he made his way up from the river, there was a sudden rustle to his left. A deer raised itself from its hiding place and now bounded away gracefully towards the relative security of the plantation. A few sheep grazing in its path, scarcely looked up from their search for something edible among the bracken. Seabirds wheeled overhead, moving inland from the storm to come.

It was a long walk back to the house. He should have brought shoes. The waders were on the heavy side and his leg was still not quite back to normal. He stopped for a moment to rest and look about him. It was so peaceful. That's why it had been such a joy to come there after the bitterness and the hate of his ill-starred mission in Iceland. His civil servant veneer of self-control had been peeled off by the criminal stupidity of his parent department that had landed him in hospital for two months. There had been no apology and he had blown his top. They had merely looked shocked and coldly extended his sick-leave. Now he was due to go back to the rat race once more and leave the peace, the hissing of the rain on the bracken and the constant rumble from the river below. The rest had done him some good, but he was still an angry man.

He walked on. As he went, he heard the sound of a car engine in the distance and wondered that it was a bit late for the Land-Rover that brought the mail. A few minutes more and the neat, whitewashed house appeared from behind its wind-break of trees. He caught a parting glimpse of a black Volkswagen as it drove out of sight over the hill road behind.

His uncle came across from the stables and met him at the gate. He was carrying a basket full of eggs.

"You're just too late, Calder. There were two men here to see you," he said. "I told them you'd be back soon, but they said they couldn't wait. They've only just gone." MacCaig noticed the worried expression on the old man's face and the uncharacteristic lack of interest in his catch.

"I'll just take these waders off first, Uncle. They're wet and heavy. I'll be through in a minute. You can tell me then." He limped towards the rear door of the house with his rod and the basket with the fish. His uncle came after him.

"Calder, listen. I'm worried. I think they were the police, though they didn't say," he said urgently. "You're not in any trouble, are you? Your aunt heard and was a bit upset too."

MacCaig laughed. "Tell her not to be. I've been here quite a while now, and there's been little local opportunity for crime."

"I'm not being humorous," the old man said slowly. He put the basket of eggs carefully down on the doorstep beside him.

"Tell me about it then. What did they want?"

"Both the men were dressed unseasonably and in dark suits," he said, as if that explained everything. "I asked them who they were, and they wouldn't say at first. They just asked when you'd be back. I felt that if they were going to be taciturn, I could outdo them on that." MacCaig smiled back understandingly. "Then they said it was about some land they wanted to buy. They said they were representing a firm of Glasgow solicitors."

"And naturally you wondered when I had suddenly become a landowner without your knowing all about it, and that if they were police and were after me, why they hadn't equipped themselves with a more convincing story," MacCaig interjected.

"How did you know?" the old man said. Then he saw the glint in MacCaig's eye. "Aye, you're making fun of me again, Calder. But I'm serious, I'm telling you."

"Sorry, Uncle. No offence. Then they left?" MacCaig asked.

Having teased the old man routinely over his curiosity, he was now genuinely intrigued to know who his visitors had been.

"I said I knew where to find you. I have really no wish to pry into your affairs, but eventually they didn't really seem to want to meet you at all. It was distinctly odd."

"And there was no message?"

"No. Not a message exactly . . ." The other man was being deliberately slow now.

"Out with it, Uncle." MacCaig forced a smile out of his growing irritation.

"As I said, they started by telling me it was about some land they wanted to buy. Then, while they were waiting, they started questioning me about what you were doing here. When I told them that you had been recuperating and hadn't left here for months, they seemed very surprised. They whispered to each other for a bit, then one of them said rather rudely that they had changed their minds and they wouldn't bother you after all."

"And that was all?"

"Yes, except that as they were getting into their car, and by that time they seemed to be in a hurry to get away and avoid meeting you, I heard one of them say something to the effect that someone had got it wrong and that you couldn't have anything to do with the Norsemen."

"With *the Norsemen*? Sorry. What was that?"

"That's right, the Norsemen. I heard the name clearly enough. You know. It'll be that lunatic fringe of the Nationalists who not only want to throw out the English but to bring in the Scandinavians at the same time."

MacCaig now realised what his uncle was talking about. He remembered seeing a press report which had hinted that some group of people were trying to form a sort of European federalist movement with that name, and that they had been canvassing support from the Nationalists. He hadn't paid much attention at the time.

"They're a peculiar lot, you know." His uncle went on.

"Lunatic fringe, but apparently just that little better organised than the usual run of political movements."

"How d'you know all this? You seem to be well informed."

"You forget I have an occasional round of golf with MacKenzie of the Glasgow C.I.D. He was probably speaking out of turn but he told me that the authorities are worried about this group, and are keeping a watchful eye on them."

The old man paused thoughtfully when he saw the reaction his words had produced. MacCaig had turned away and was scowling heavily in the direction the Volkswagen had taken. Inwardly, he was cursing his Department for going back to their game-playing again. It *must* have been to do with them. That was the trouble with them, sitting smugly on the fringes of the Civil Service, jumping at any chance to play cops and robbers anytime a new movement emerged that they didn't like. They had 'phoned just yesterday telling him to report back for duty. They had talked about a new assignment, when all he wanted was a quiet desk job. But they didn't need to send men for him as well. He would come, come reluctantly, but he would come.

He turned suddenly and forced another smile. "Do you think we can persuade my aunt to put on the kettle for a cup of tea, Uncle? I'm freezing after the fishing," he said quietly. "And you haven't even asked about my salmon. But we'll have to be quick. I have the ferry to catch."

Whitehall, Tuesday Afternoon

"Come on then, Philip. Let's have it. Bring in the files. How many feet high is my in-tray?"

"About two, Minister." The Private Secretary was precise.

"Where is it then?"

"That's what I've been trying to say, Minister. The P.M. wants you round at the Cabinet Office in half an hour. I hardly thought it worth it."

"What the hell? Why? . . . Why can't the Secretary of State go?"

"He's got to answer questions in the House this afternoon, you remember, and in any case, as far as I can gather, the P.M. has asked for you specially. The Secretary of State is, well, you know what I mean."

The Minister did know. It was common knowledge. His Ministerial superior had rather given up of late, bowing out of the political limelight as much as he could. The wave of Nationalist by-elections had started the rot and now there was this press campaign. It was the current gossip that he was to be sacrificed on the block of political expediency. If today's Lochinver by-election also went to the Nationalists, it could only be a matter of days.

"Poor Arthur. He's done his best." The Minister always spoke his mind to his P.S. Otherwise what was the good of having one. And Philip had always proved a loyal confidant. "O.K. What's on the agenda?"

"I'm afraid I don't know, Minister. At least we haven't been officially told," the P.S. explained unhappily. He always tried to keep his Minister fully in the picture. It paid dividends. Some Private Secretaries acted as filters and only told their Ministers what they thought was good for them. He played it the other way.

"It's a specially arranged Cabinet Committee. They are a funny . . . I mean unusual lot of Ministers attending."

"So you know a little unofficially, is that it? You Civil Servants hang together like clay or something. Come on now, Philip. What's the gossip?"

"Well, it's something to do with the Nationalists."

"I presume that's why I'm invited."

"But the Foreign Secretary and the Defence Secretary are coming too. I hear the business in Oslo is to be discussed."

"What business?"

"The bomb attack and the British businessman who was killed."

"Oh yes, I read about it at the weekend. What's going on?"

"They really wouldn't say, Minister. I did try, but they wouldn't . . . not on the 'phone."

"I see. It's like that is it. Not on the 'phone."

Earls Court, Wednesday Morning

There were four of them, three men and the girl, Fiona Ross. The sound of the television was turned down fairly low which didn't matter too much since none of them wanted to listen. The programme was inane in the extreme and the political compère was visibly tired. It was almost two in the morning and still the result of the Lochinver by-election hadn't come through. Normally the result in this remote constituency would not have been declared till the middle of the following day, but such was the press interest that the local returning officers had been persuaded to draft in extra assistance, and the result had been promised by now.

There wasn't much left to say. The team of experts, roped together to comment on the result, had played their last cliché; one of them, a Professor of Politics, was obviously drunk; the crowds outside Lochinver town hall had been scanned continuously for the past hour and the programme producer was getting desperate.

The four in the room weren't too worried. They had the confidence of victory. Each of them was very different, but they all shared the same conviction and the same expressed wish to be in Lochinver with the impatient crowd, rather than in a bed-sitter in Earl's Court.

The room was almost in darkness, lit only by the television screen and the dim flickering from an old-fashioned gas fire. They kept it that way not for any more immediate reason than because it drew less attention to the shabbiness of the room, the brown discoloured wallpaper, the scruffy furniture, and the peeling paint on the ceiling. An unexpectedly fresh bunch of flowers on a table by the window and a stark red and black election poster fixed with drawing pins to the centre of one wall, were the only attempts at more recent decoration.

Fiona Ross had produced a half bottle of whisky. Until then they had been on beer but the same glasses served for both. Calder MacCaig sat slouched in a battered arm chair, tumbler in hand, staring at the flickering screen. The others had tried to talk to him at first but he had simply grunted at them and from then on they ignored him, discussing quietly among themselves. Only the girl glanced at him from time to time as he sat readjusting sullenly to London after the peace of his months of recuperation in the north.

He had caught the afternoon plane down and had rung his Department immediately. A secretary with a high-pitched, well-bred voice, informed him that the Director of Operations was away and wouldn't be able to see him till Friday. That had been a bad start after the telephone call, the messengers in their black Volkswagen, and the rush to get back on time. Muttering imprecations, he had slammed down the receiver angrily and had gone off in search of a drink. Later, ending up where he knew he'd find friends, he had stayed with them to watch the result.

As from a distance, he watched the other three, all friends or acquaintances from University days. Callum, small, dark and Celtic, a poet and a dreamer; a product of one of the remoter Scottish islands who kept his deeply held political passions well under control, seldom or never breaking away from his pattern of reason and slow-moving good sense. No leader of men, yet because he was the sort of person who acted as a kind of perpetual keeper of the common conscience, he was seldom far from the centre of his own range of political activity.

Beside him sat Axel the schemer, bearded and intense, but with an extraordinary intellect and energy. A man who during his University career had cast aside his reputed Scandinavian background to adopt with an almost savage dedication, the cause of Scottish Nationalism. He had outshone the most extreme militants with the effort he put into the organisation, despising the dreamers who tried to follow the same course, yet, as he said, stayed swathed in their kilts and ridiculous historical myths. His very drive made him acceptable despite his total lack of Scottish blood. Nationalism, he would argue, was an international phenomenon, and this had led him as it had led Callum, to seek new political horizons.

Then there was Fiona Ross. She too had found common cause with them. Fiona the research student, dark long hair, attractive rather than pretty, strong willed but gentle.

He had drawn so much away from her and from them all and their ways of life, ever since that April day in his final University year when he had been approached and offered a job which, he was told, was exciting and out of the ordinary. Looking forward only as far as his finals at the time, he had been non-committal, but they had come back to him after his graduation and before he had had time to find anything better to do. They said he was just the sort of man they were looking for, and he was flattered. He had taken them up on their offer and in many ways it had suited him right from the start. And now? Now he had a sort of love-hate relationship with his work, with more hate than love in it.

MacCaig pulled himself from his dream with a start. The others had been talking softly about their politics as they waited for the result. Sharing many of their sympathies, he had nonetheless withdrawn himself as always from involvement, partly from habit of being a Civil Servant, partly from inclination. He had heard them talking about European alliances and the need for new groupings, and had listened with only half an ear. But then suddenly he caught the word "Norsemen" repeated softly once, perhaps twice. He leaned forward to listen, to join in, to ask their meaning of the word he had heard before. But before he could speak, Fiona Ross was hushing everyone and pointing at the television.

"Yes, I think the returning officer is coming forward now." The T.V. announcer's relieved voice blended with the sound of shouting from Lochinver's town square. Arc lights and cameras were focused on the Victorianate balcony. Too many people seemed to be standing there by the big windows, trying to get in on the act. The Provost, doubling as returning officer, stepped forward and held up his hands for silence. He began to read from a piece of paper he held in his hand. One could see he was nervous.

THREE

Westminster, Wednesday Morning

The Minister stretched uncomfortably in the narrow bed. Most of the clothes seemed to have slipped to the floor. He braved the cold long enough to put an arm out and retrieve them, but it didn't work. He switched on the bedside light and looked at his watch: 7.15 a.m., and a bitter February day.

Why the hell wasn't the heating on? He paid enough for this pokey so-called bachelor flat. It wasn't good enough. He was a Minister of the Crown after all—even though a junior one. That was the trouble with this schizophrenic existence. A *pied à terre* within four minutes of the House and yet expected to have an established house up in his constituency, four hundred miles away. No wonder many of his colleagues lived so totally divided a life that divorce was commonplace among them. They *must* be able to find him somewhere better.

He got up, put on a towelling dressing gown and found his slippers scattered under the bed. Yes, he'd get something better, and then maybe he'd be able to persuade his wife to bring the baby and spend the occasional week in London. Maybe. She didn't like to be separated from the house and the dog, and she was magnificent at keeping in touch with the constituents. In very many ways it suited them both.

He put the kettle on in the tiny kitchen and then went to the front door. *The Times* was there already, along with a bundle of other papers. The later editions already carried the Lochinver result. Just as he had expected. The figures were a bit worse if anything. He was glad he hadn't bothered to wait up to watch it come in.

Pulling his dressing gown even tighter round him he removed some books from an easy chair, sat down and turned to *The Times* centre-page editorials. They were on about poor old

Arthur. He was going. There was no doubt about that now. The editorial listed the possible candidates for his job. He saw his own name among them, but one of his more senior colleagues was favourite, and besides, the editorial read, it was said that he himself was not too keen on taking it on. Too bloody right. He had made that known in the lobbies. Some of his colleagues, who knew him less well, believed that this declared lack of interest in the job was a sham, since it didn't match the ambition which was said to lie behind the smile. Others who perhaps knew him a little better, saw that the cap fitted well. An unpopular Ministry, with little chance allowed the incumbent to better the situation, was hardly attractive despite the Cabinet rank that came with it. Whoever took the post realised only too soon that the title of Secretary of State carried with it the dubious honour of being the focal point of all local discontent with the Government of the day. *The Times* editorial called it a challenge. It wasn't the sort the Minister wanted. Especially at present, with the Nationalists so much on the make, it was political suicide, the kiss of death for someone in his position.

Besides, he had been aware for a long time of a different ambition underlying his own thinking, not just in political terms, more emotional, more personal. He had always admitted that he was an out-and-out political animal who had never fought shy of the constant intra-Party struggles and conspiracies. His closer, more percipient colleagues knew he still had personal aims which he hadn't quite managed to conceal as a hankering after Celtic emotionalism. While he had no truck with narrow nationalism now, he had never quite known where he stood on "King and Country". It was, rather, a simple realisation that things changed, and if he was to survive, he must change too. Empires and Commonwealths collapsed as a matter of course, but so from time to time did States. Nothing could be permanent, except, in a general way, races, tribes, ethnic groups. He hadn't thought it all out with any precision, but it was just that people seemed to take for granted that "the Country" was something fixed for all time. Why? Take

Germany. It had only been united—whatever that meant—from 1871 to 1944. If the political winds were blowing in the direction of new, broader concepts of nationalism, then he must watch to see that he came down on the right side, able to keep his options open. And what was wrong with guarded opportunism? When the first of the new nationalists had been elected to the Commons, he had been genuinely enthusiastic. He had even sponsored an early one who had lacked fellow party men to assist him to his seat. The antipathy shown by some older members of the established parties was far from shared by him. It was the excitement of the new and the memories of old ideas which lingered on inside him, despite the careful weeding to which he had subjected his ideals over the years. But it wasn't out of opportunism alone nor from the understandable wish to save his political future that he didn't want the job. For there were other, much less public reasons as well.

The Minister went through into his tiny bathroom, switched on the light above the mirror, and began to shave, slowly and carefully as always. It was the most relaxing time in his whole day, the time when he could think without being disturbed by constant interruption. The hot water refreshed and relaxed his skin and the new blade gently eased away yesterday's problems along with the stubble. He finished, wiped and dried his face and then picked up his silver-backed hairbrushes and methodically began to attack his mop of greying hair. The political world might quite soon begin anew for him. He smiled reassuringly at his restored image in the glass.

The bell rang. He went to the door, pulling his dressing gown around him. The milkman to be paid. No small change. Would a five pound note . . .? O.K. leave it till next week. *God*, it was cold.

Pall Mall, Wednesday Lunchtime

"This place is getting dreadfully crowded. A revolt of the masses against canteen food, and one can't blame them. I'll have to go back to pies and pints at the pub if it goes on." Rossetti looked round with distaste at the plastic-panelled basement cafeteria of his once-celebrated gentlemen's club, and then returned to shovelling large quantities of mashed potato into his mouth. There was silence for a few minutes. His companion was bored but equally determined not to stir things up by filling the sound gap.

A waitress, with liberal samples of the day's menu scattered across her diminutive white apron, thumped two plates of something coated in bright yellow custard down beside them. A plastic menu holder and a folded card which announced the acceptability of luncheon vouchers, cascaded on to the floor as she made room for the dishes.

"But I haven't finished my meat course." Rossetti looked up in horror. "Please could you bring it back in a few minutes?" The woman swept the plates away again with a look of remarkable malice. She left the other items on the floor.

"Well that's the pud' for today," the companion giggled. Rossetti looked pained.

"No loss. Have a cigarillo? No? You don't mind if I do? Now where was I? Yes, it's getting enthralling. I wish I could get to the bottom of it." He lowered his voice conspiratorially.

"Anyway, this Cabinet Committee," he went on, "according to my informant—you know young Wilmott, the one in A.G.P., not his brother—it apparently broke up in disorder. No decisions, nothing. . . . Half of them didn't believe the story about where the Norsemen get their money; the other half felt it was the end of everything. The P.M. is reputedly most perturbed, most. He himself was sitting astride the breach as usual. Then both sides walked away. It must have been rather painful."

"Coffee?" said the waitress. It was a challenge. The two men, united for an instant, decided not to mention the missing cherry tart with custard. Once was enough with the coffee already on the table.

"Thank you so much, . . . and the bill please. Just when

you've time of course." There was no hiding the weakness in the voice.

"Yes, they've been getting these reports for months. Someone's been burying them away on a file. On the first of the series someone had just written 'Nonsense'. At first they tried to blame me for having suppressed them. Ridiculous, but I had a hard time convincing them it wasn't. It wasn't even my writing. I suspect Wyndham-Brown, you know the man who had that heart attack recently, poor chap. The P.M.'s angry about that. But as Wyndham-Brown's dead now, even he can't do anything about it. I can understand the P.M. of course. Despite his trying to compromise, he's really terribly worried, perhaps not so much about the business itself, but the effect it's having on the Cabinet."

"Together? That's one pound sixty-seven and a half." The waitress appeared and menaced again.

"How did it come to that? We both had the same and there are no farthings in the new currency."

"If you've a complaint, the Head Waiter is . . ."

Rossetti paid, and they stood up to go.

"To top it all," he said in a whisper, "even when the Committee was told that it was one of our best men that had landed under that grenade, some still weren't convinced. You see, it wasn't the Embassy that was being attacked at all. It's all very surprising, isn't it?"

His companion didn't look at all surprised since he hadn't been listening. Rossetti stared at him sharply for a moment and then, with a slightly pained expression on his face, walked quickly out of the dining room.

L.S.E. Wednesday Afternoon

The students were demonstrating again outside the main gates. It wasn't clear to Fiona Ross what was at issue this time, but she knew that it wouldn't be in aid of her particular cause. Some of these people couldn't see what was going on in front of their noses. They used their vigour in aid of injustice in some far corner of the globe which was all very well. But there were things closer to home.

She pushed through the crowd towards the Refectory. They all looked so scruffy. Why was this apparent lack of cleanliness and the shabby clothes the order of the day? She would never advocate that people should conform, wear ties, that sort of thing. But the shabbiness of the demonstrators, the studied down-and-outness, that itself was a sort of mediocre conformity.

She herself, long dark hair neatly pulled back from her face, a well proportioned figure set off rather than camouflaged by her clothes, was the sort of girl that men noticed not because she was strikingly beautiful, but by reason of her poise and controlled charm. In herself, she felt she had been rather successful in managing to break away from her staid background of a childhood and school years in an Army family. Her father, the Colonel of the Regiment, had never opposed but certainly had failed to understand her subsequent involvement in both academic and political life. But now she was in a slightly superior position as a post-graduate student in the final stages of writing a Doctoral Thesis on Nineteenth Century social legislation, which was why she was working in a town that she actively disliked rather than in the North. Now that part of her rebellion against her upbringing was over and nonconformity for its own sake was a thing of the past, she still reacted against any tendency to become too stuffy about how other younger people lived and behaved.

She saw her two colleagues at their usual table in the alcove. So Calder hadn't come after all. She felt a shiver of disappointment that her invitation to him to come and find out more about the Norsemen hadn't been taken up. Waving a greeting, she queued up at the self-service counter, got herself a coffee, and then went over to join them.

Callum was looking vague as usual, and beside him, Axel. Empty coffee cups littered the table along with a cheap tin ashtray filled with butts.

"He hasn't come then?"

"There are more important things than that," said Axel, scowling at her through his beard.

"The money?"

"No. That's come through all right. With it, however, has come the message that we've to start."

"But I thought . . ." started Fiona.

"No. I mean really start. It's all got to be carefully synchronised. We'll have to watch out from now on. We're not up against amateurs and they'll know pretty soon what's at stake."

Again she wondered about Axel. Callum was meant to be in charge of the London end, the publicity, the public relations. But it was Axel with the permanent gleam in his eye who always took the lead. Just as he was now sitting with a folder of papers in front of him, efficiently sifting through letters, reports, agendas, like a business tycoon. He was in a different league, a professional among amateurs. She could easily imagine him with a staff of secretaries and other aides sitting at the hub of some large industrial complex—or perhaps more realistically—some octupus-like government Ministry, since Axel was an avowed opponent of large-scale private enterprise.

"The posters . . .? Good. And you've got the handouts for the Press saying where the spokesman can be reached?" Axel shot his questions at them in turn.

"Good," he said again. "It's no longer a schoolboy lark, you know. As soon as it gets really under way we're going to meet with the real opposition." He stood up to go. "Tomorrow at the same time." It was an order not a question. Fiona looked at Callum.

"Yes," said Callum. He watched almost disinterestedly as Axel walked away towards the Refectory door.

It was the two vague idealists that were left, Fiona thought. It had all been a great dream. She remembered the early undergraduate days filled with a romantic attraction towards nationalism and independence, being honest enough to admit that, in its very earliest stages, these emotions were closely tied up with her more personal feelings for one of the leading men in the movement. Then there had been the more politically inspired excitements of hotly contested elections and the occasional flush of victory. Later, she and a few others felt they saw the problems and possibilities of nationalism in a colder and less emotional light and had realised that no nation, especially one trying to break away from a long established Union of Crowns and Parliaments, could exist entirely on its own, answerable to no one. It had to look for new allies but ones of its own choosing. The Norsemen concept with its policies of drawing together the Northern countries of Europe whose cultures and historical ties often had more in common with each other than with their southern neighbours, had been enormously compelling. But now when it meant real action. . . . It was exciting of course, but then they had to begin looking at the future, what it all really meant, and to whom.

"So Calder didn't come," she said once again.

"I didn't really think he would," said Callum. "He has his pension to think about."

"That's not quite fair." Fiona felt herself colouring slightly and knew that Callum would notice.

"But let's leave Calder out of it for the moment," Callum added quietly. "As Axel said, there are bigger things at stake. Yes, the money's come in, and a large amount of it at that. The source must be pretty well-off. We ourselves haven't been able to raise a quarter of the amount in a year."

"Where is it?" she asked.

"Axel . . ." Callum made a vague gesture.

Fiona had guessed. The others on the Committee always appeared so uncurious about where the money had come from and about a lot of other things as well. Because the cause was great they didn't question motives. They didn't realise that money could be tied.

Axel, the efficient spider at the centre of the web, twitching the threads, controlling, regulating. She had long thought of him like that, ever since he had tried to twitch her into bed with him, expecting her to come running, fitting into her precise place like everything else in his scheme of things. But she hadn't reacted to the summons, not from any moral scruples but because her independent nature refused to allow her to be dictated to, nor to become any one man's chattel. In the past, her affairs had been short, intense, but entirely of her own choosing, and with a personality, figure and restrained sensuality which were equally attractive to men, she had had little difficulty in retaining the initiative. This time there had been a nasty and embarrassing scene with Axel. Eventually they had got back on speaking terms and they worked well enough together now, except that she was wary of him and he, perhaps covering up his failure, tended to treat her with less respect than in more detached circumstances, he might have allowed her. Appreciating this, she tried to disassociate her personal feelings of dislike from her respect for his efficiency and she still ended up with the spider image. If only Callum were more definite, or . . . or if Calder had come.

She finished her coffee slowly, staring emptily across the Refectory. Callum sat silently beside her. Eventually they both stood up to go.

After they had left, a little man in a blue duffel jacket—older than the common run of students—drifted casually up to the table they had vacated. He pulled a copy of the *Guardian* out of his pocket and began to read. Then he appeared to change his mind and stood up again. As he did so, he detached a small black box from its magnetic hold on one of the metal table legs and put it carefully into his pocket.

FOUR

Oslo, Thursday Morning

The man they called Stefan Issouna was standing by the big double-glazed window staring out at the fir trees. There was little else to look at except the fir trees and an occasional silver birch. Away in the distance, however, were the roofs of brightly painted wooden houses with, by each one, the inevitable thin whiteness of a flag-pole. On the skyline showed the intermittent glimpse of the fjord. With the dullness of the morning, the scene had lost any winter charm. There had been no recent falls and the snow had almost entirely disappeared from the trees, with little to relieve their heavy green. A few patches of brown, moss-covered gravel were beginning to show through the iced snow on the drive.

"The trouble with our language is that while it only takes a few weeks to master the grammar, it takes a lifetime to learn to pronounce."

Issouna turned round slowly from the window to face the speaker. He ignored the remark.

"It's now over five days since . . ." His anger showed through clearly enough. He had disliked and distrusted the other man from the beginning.

"I'm sorry, I don't know what more I can do."

"You can ring, Herr Schoeyen. There is a telephone, I presume?"

"Yes, but to whom?"

"That's your affair, Herr Schoeyen. You are paid to know such things."

"All right. I'll try." The door closed noisily and Issouna turned back to his view from the window.

He was nervous, which for him was unusual. His size normally did not permit excitement. Now an even glow of perspiration coated his forehead. He reached into his pocket and produced a large silk handkerchief with which he gently patted his brow. They had turned the central heating up too high again. Why did he always have to repeat himself? He hated incompetence and that man Schoeyen was chaotic by any standards. He walked irritably over to a bell-push by the fireplace and pressed. A minute later, when no one had appeared, he pressed again and this time he kept his finger on the knob.

The door opened and Schoeyen came into the room.

"There's no use ringing like that, Stefan. The servants are all out at the moment and I'm trying to telephone to find out. One thing at a bloody time." The door was shut violently.

Back to the window, the fir trees and the flag-poles. A visitor not appreciating the national significance of the flag-pole to Norwegians, might have been forgiven for believing that every house was obliged by law to have one. Common, but not as common as the trees, trees like a wall of silence shutting everything in and everything out. Snow, trees, snow—Ibsen alone had caught the feeling. An aeroplane droned unseen overhead, coming in to land at the airport a couple of miles away. To the man it reflected the prospect of getting out, of going back home. There the winter would almost be over by now and there would be no need for central heating.

He felt a dribble of sweat form under his chin and mechanically brushed it away with a fleshy hand. Not that he kept any sentimental attachment to his homeland. At one time in the past he had prided himself on his lack of attachment to anyone, to anything. Now he had ceased to think about it. With remarkable intellectual honesty, he admitted to himself that he now rendered lip-service to a creed only because they paid to use his professional skills. Many men, nominally more loyal and patriotic than he, were less honest about their mercenary motives. This thought was a perpetual reassurance to him.

The door opened again.

"No joy. But they did promise to ring back. It seems that they've put a complete blanket down. It's going to be difficult, Stefan," Schoeyen said.

"You know when my plane is. I must know by then that there was no mistake, that death was instantaneous, that he didn't have a chance to talk. Get back to that 'phone, or better go yourself. But before you go, turn down the confounded heating. I'm being cooked alive."

"But it's quite cool . . . ." Schoeyen stopped in the middle of his words when he saw the sweat on the heavy face. "Right you are. But as to going in myself, it's a bit risky, isn't it? Our orders were to stay clear."

"That's because you told us you had a contact lined up. They thought you had it properly fixed. They won't be pleased. Now, as far as orders go—I'm giving them from now on. Go, and don't come back till you find out."

"You can't speak to me like that, here in my own house. You're here on sufferance. I shall . . ." Again Schoeyen saw the big man's face and hesitated.

"O.K. Sorry, Stefan. You're right. I'll go straight away. It shouldn't be too difficult. The papers probably have the details on it by now. I'll speak to . . ."

"Go!"

"Right. Don't get all worked up." The door slammed shut once again. Issouna winced at the sound, produced his silk handkerchief once again and wiped his brow. Before returning it to his pocket he looked at it in disgust. It was crushed and quite damp.

"Damnation!" he suddenly exclaimed and rushed to the door. He pulled it open roughly. "The central heating, damn you!" he bellowed. But his words were drowned by the sound of a car driving quickly away through the pines.

Whitehall, Thursday Afternoon

It was a beautiful oval room. The Georgian plasterwork on the ceiling had been picked out in white against a pale blue background, like a piece of Wedgwood. Naked, well-built nymphs pursued unreluctant shepherds across the frieze on the almost flawless white marble of the mantelpiece. Above it hung the portrait of an eighteenth-century nobleman resplendent in ermine and lace, whose large and regal gun-dog standing at his feet looked considerably more intelligent than its master. Comfortable red leather armchairs were scattered round the room, and in the centre stood the magnificent mahogany desk with its silver inkwells and trays. Only the imposing row of red and green telephones on the desk were there to indicate that times had changed.

If he had accepted, this room would have been one of the principal joys. The P.M. had pressed him hard, as he had known he would. The more senior colleagues, which *The Times* had mentioned in its editorial, hadn't been too interested in the job either. And while the P.M. had said he understood the reasons for the refusal, the Minister wasn't too sure about that. The P.M. wasn't too good on people having consciences. He was right enough; they *were* a burden to those in power.

It was a pity. At any other time he would have jumped at the chance. And it had been made clear to him that if he refused, there wouldn't be any other jobs with a seat in the Cabinet for a long time. He had taken it as it was meant—as a threat. But for once the Minister was adamant, sure in the belief of where his political bread was going to be buttered in the future, and the P.M. hadn't wasted any more time on him. It was typical, the ridiculous way he had straight away got landed with the other business. He was just leaving the study when the P.M. had called him back.

"I want you to take over the investigation of the Norsemen business for the meantime, at least until I can find someone to take over as Secretary. You will, won't you? I, *we all,* would be sorry to lose your services."

It was clear as crystal. Take it or go. Weakly, he had taken it.

"You needn't worry about your public position. It's not like the other appointment. You just stay in your present job and you keep your political options open. No one will know."

The P.M. had been openly sneering at him. That was the trouble. Any slight deviation from the party line was branded as dangerous fence-sitting. The Minister hadn't liked it. And they both knew that if the Norsemen thing became a successful political movement, his own position as its castigator would soon leak out. He wouldn't be able to back down. It was as if the P.M. had said he couldn't care a damn for his principles nor his ambitions.

So that was that. But he could use the room for the moment. Clasping his hands leisurely behind his head, he swung round from the desk in the big swivel chair to gaze out of the curved windows. It was raining and the trees in the park beyond looked washed out like a pale water-colour. Two identical men in bowler hats, black umbrellas precisely vertical, like swords, walked in step across the Parade to the archway. Men from the Defence Ministry. Left, right, left, right, left. . . .

Now what? Phase one: reconcile ideals, vague ambitions based on Celtic twilightism and all the rest of that rubbish, with the job in hand. Phase two: . . .? Wait. Get phase one out of the way first.

Put aside that a Northern Alliance, a Nordic Union, might make just as much long-term sense as a European Market or Federation. Put aside that, for historical and geographical reasons, it might work better than an Atlantic Alliance and that he could be in on it from the start. Put the Norsemen idea aside because it cuts across established state structure, but more so because it's not what it seems. Not what it seems. . . . "It's not that I'm against the principle of the thing," the P.M. had said. That was a lie for a start. The fact that it had, or they said that it had, been infiltrated by "undesirable elements" was almost irrelevant. Or was it? Was it a possible excuse, a way out of a dilemma over principles? The Minister saw and then took the easy way as he had done before in his career. Losing out on a top job once in a day over a question of principle was quite enough. *Infiltration*, that was the key.

He reached for pen and paper. A political movement was one thing, a conspiracy was another. An unusually hard look crept over his face.

Whitehall, Thursday Evening

"He's clever, the P.M. is. Have you heard who he's got to take over the whole operation? If you can't beat them, make sure you're on the same side." Rossetti leapt rapidly across the room like a ballet dancer, and then pirouetted around, a fraction before colliding with a heavy steel filing cabinet. A security poster, loosely sellotaped to the wall, fluttered slightly as he passed. It showed a very dubious man with a beard eavesdropping on two pinstriped Civil Servants gossiping in a pub. Its motto ran: *It's pointless shutting your safe if that's all you shut: Keep the Nation's Secrets Secret.* Rossetti scowled at it and at the room in general. Unthinkingly, he produced a penknife from his pocket and waved it in the air like a conductor's baton.

"It's all got beyond a joke," he went on. "Students and demonstrations, posters and a bit of high talk, but behind it, dangerous forces at work. Nasty. Very nasty." He walked back across the office linoleum from the filing cabinet, and swirled round again to face his audience. None of them looked up from their desks. They had their work to do. Rossetti shrugged. It didn't matter too much.

The telephone on his desk gave a discreet purr. He leapt across to his desk.

"Extension 471 . . . Yes, speaking. Oh yes indeed. Right away Minister. No, I have the files with me now. Yes . . . five minutes. Certainly Sir." He put the receiver down respectfully and glanced up at his colleagues. They were, for once, looking at him with a certain amount of interest. He took his advantage, said nothing and walked swiftly out of the room. That would teach them.

Rossetti told the story later. It had been very nasty, he said. He had gone along the green painted corridors to the lift, then down to the ground floor. The ancient lift operative, he remembered, had been less than polite as he had screeched the gates open for him. He had paused briefly at Reception to make a quick telephone call, explaining pompously to the

Receptionist that a summons by the Minister might, at that late hour, mean that he'd be late for his dinner engagement. It was a dreadful nuisance. What one did for one's country . . . Then he had left the building, past the security guards and out into the fresh air.

One of these interminable demonstrations was under way. The police were stretched in a thin line at the end of Downing Street to keep the noise from the inner sanctum. He could have gone round the back, but that would have meant being late for the Minister. It wasn't far. It would, he had thought, be all right. They looked a fairly amiable group of demonstrators this time, though doubtless unwashed as usual. He had grasped the briefcase containing the files closely to him and made for the row of police.

"Could I get through, Officer? Rather a rush. Sorry." The policeman had let him through and he was swirled up in the crowd.

He had pushed his way on. It was difficult going, as he was fighting against the human tide that was trying to get to Downing Street. He had pushed past some girl students in black oilskins. Quite pretty some of them . . . "Watch where you're going, beautiful" some bearded man had shouted after him. He ignored the cat-call. He was nearly through the crowd.

Then his legs were pulled from under him. Someone must have been on his hands and knees in the crowd. He had felt himself falling. Two or three pale intense male faces round him and then, darkness.

Then he was inside a van. There had been a nurse and a policeman.

"That'll teach you to take part in demonstrations. You feeling a bit better?" the officer had asked. "Nasty tear you've got in your jacket. You ought to know better. Lucky you're not getting charged. O.K., what's your name?"

Rossetti had felt far from elegant. He had felt sick. He saw the blood and dirt on his hands, and the broken nails. Then he had remembered the Minister.

"My briefcase?" he asked in a panic.

"What are you on about?" said the policeman. "I asked you for your name."

Rossetti had searched in his inside pocket and produced his identity card. The officer's tone changed at once. He stood up smartly. "Oh dear," he had said." It's like that, is it. I'll put a radio call through straight away, Sir? . . . And a message to the Minister's office? Of course, Sir."

Rossetti had felt in his pocket. He had even lost his comb. Yes, it had been unpleasant.

Whitehall, Friday Afternoon

"It's your own choice. I could add that it wouldn't be if I had my way," the Director of Operations said.

"It's kind of you to be so open."

"Sarcasm won't help in these circumstances, Calder."

"I'm sorry. I find it very difficult. You don't seem to . . ."

"But I do understand very well, Calder. That's the point. You have a decision to make, and quickly."

"Can't I be put on some other job?"

"Escapism. No, it's my turn to be sorry. I shouldn't have said that. Conflicts of loyalties are never happy things. People have had to face them in the past too, you know."

"That's just what I'm saying." MacCaig jumped up out of the deep mock-leather chair and limped across to the older man's desk. He scowled down at him but the Director didn't move.

"After the Iceland business, it was a case of two month's hospital and then three further months up in Scotland. You send for me, and I come back at once. Then you spring this whole new business on me. You know how I feel. These Nationalist victories mean something to me. I've never hidden the fact. And yet you obviously don't even trust me to come when you ask, but have to send two of the men to see that I come. I've always played this game quite honestly. I would have told you if I hadn't been coming. In any case I didn't know that you wanted me for this."

"Wait a bit, wait a bit. Not so fast, Calder. One thing at a time. We have the fullest trust—and I don't know what you're talking about. I never sent any men to get you. You've worked long enough with us to know we don't work that way. Trust is the essence of this business." The Director stood up and faced him. "What two men?" he asked suddenly.

"I . . . er . . . There were two men." MacCaig was taken off his guard. Were they playing some game with him? He had grown bitterly over-suspicious since the let-down in Iceland. But they didn't usually play that way. The Director was right.

"Two men came to my uncle's farm the other day. In a Volkswagen. They were looking for me. They said it was about the Norsemen. I had hardly heard the name mentioned before you told me and I know nothing about it as an organisation. I assumed . . ."

"I see. Well you assumed wrongly. It wasn't us. And what conclusions do you draw, Calder?"

"If it really wasn't you, then it means that someone's security is a bit lax."

"Could be. We've had some files taken and the man who was carrying them was bumped on the head. Your name appeared frequently on the files as the person who is to run the Norsemen to earth. Perhaps it wasn't obvious to the other side that you didn't, that you weren't yet in the picture yourself." The Director laughed briefly.

"I heard about the files," said MacCaig coldly. "But that's not really a good enough explanation. They were only taken yesterday, and my visitors called on the day before that."

The Director frowned slightly and made a note on a pad in front of him. "I see. Then I'll look into it further but meanwhile there is one other thing: you said just now that you knew nothing about the Norsemen until I told you?"

"That's not strictly true. I had heard some chatter."

"When you were sitting round the television early on Wednesday morning?"

"So you *have* been watching me. I've bloody well had enough, I can tell you. I've made my decision." MacCaig exploded.

"Wait a bit. Not so fast. We weren't watching you. You just

came into the field of fire quite by chance. It was quite a surprise for us. Some of us thought that you might have joined them. I had to fight for your name."

"You might have been badly let down."

"I guessed as much."

"And why not? I'm my own master. I have as much right to join up with them as with . . . the . . . the European Federalists." He was furious now. He would go in a moment, before anything happened.

"The Federalists haven't started bumping people off so far."

"What are you suggesting? The Norsemen set-up as far as I can see is going to develop into a perfectly reasonable political movement. There are good and genuine people involved. Don't start smear tactics just because the *status quo* may be a little upset."

The Director looked almost relieved at the reaction he had produced. Things hadn't gone too far yet.

"No one is using smear tactics, Calder. I know well that there are good and genuine people involved."

"But the Establishment just doesn't like it. Is that it?"

The Director picked up a folder almost without seeming to think. He looked straight and hard at Calder MacCaig and said: "I was hoping that I wouldn't have to persuade you. Now I see I must. Your Scottish renaissance seems to have gone too far. Well here are a few facts."

"I don't want . . ."

"Sit down and listen. Go on, sit down, I said."

The two men glared at each other across the desk top. Then they both sat down.

"You remember Tinker?"

"Of course I do. You know that. It would have been a lot longer than two months in bed if it hadn't been for him. What's the game?"

"Tinker's dead."

"What? How?" MacCaig remembered a lot of things all at once. A heavy, usually drunken man, with a kindness . . . "What?" he repeated woodenly.

"You were friends? I'm sorry. I, we liked him too, despite his failings."

"His failings were better than most men's good qualities." The pious exclamation burst out spontaneously. "What happened?"

"The Norsemen killed him."

"Nonsense! You're lying. You're just trying to . . . to . . . " MacCaig was on his feet again.

"Sit down, Calder. Try to get a grip of yourself. Why should I lie? You would find out too soon if I did any such thing. Please. *Sit down.*"

MacCaig lapsed back into the armchair and gazed fiercely into space.

"I'm sorry," the older man repeated. "I should have broken it more gently. But you forced me."

"And how did it happen?" The question was quietly spoken, almost gentle.

"You probably read about it. A tourist under a grenade outside an Embassy in Oslo. The bomb wasn't aimed at the Embassy, but at Tinker. He was the tourist. He was on to them you see."

"On to whom? . . . the Norsemen?" MacCaig's voice had become dull and disinterested. He remembered the smiling face, pock-marked with drink. To hell with the lot. He was going home.

"Pull yourself together, Calder. Yes, on to the Norsemen, or some of them at any rate. It must have been something big, but unfortunately they got him before he could give us all the details. If you were a bit more yourself, you'd realise that you've seen it all before. An organisation with good motives, or not bad ones at any rate, then along come the infiltrators."

"Infiltrators?"

"Of course. The Norsemen have been infiltrated."

"By whom?"

"Does it matter? By those who don't like the *status quo*."

"But these *are* the Norsemen."

"You know what I mean. By those who don't like what

exists but who want to change it by force if necessary. Tell me one thing. Do you know where your friends get their money?"

"Friends?"

"Oh come now. You know what I mean. The people with you round the T.V. the other night, among others."

"They are people . . ."

". . . of good faith. Quite right, Calder. Or some of them are at any rate. Just like I said. But the money . . .? It comes like a fountain from idealists like yourself I suppose? Of course it doesn't. There's too bloody much. You wouldn't believe me if I told you how big their bank balance is."

"Probably not."

"But you won't leave here, Calder, until you're convinced who killed Tinker. That I can promise you. Thinking the way you seem to at the moment, you're too dangerous. Perhaps I should have left you to convalesce for a bit longer." The Director pressed a bell on his desk. Another man came into the room almost immediately.

"Take Calder into the security room and give him the Norslag File to read," the Director instructed. "Don't let him away till he's read it. And Calder, come and see me for a moment before you leave. I'd like just another quick word."

FIVE

Earls Court, Saturday Morning

Gaunt Victorian blocks, each one trying to outdo its neighbour in the drabness of its peeling paint; entrances littered with unwashed milk bottles and plastic bags of refuse, and beside each doorway, rows of anonymous bell-pushes. It was the heart of bedsitter land.

Fiona Ross went down to the end of the bleak, tenemented street, turned through a narrow passageway, and into a cobbled yard. The corrugated iron gates slid shut.

The building she was looking for was two stories high, built of wood which stood out oddly in the red brick surroundings. A small out-building to the left had a cracked notice labelled "Office". There were some wooden stairs up the outside of the building and at the top stood the printer, a big man with a bushy untidy beard.

"Are you looking for Callum?" he shouted down at Fiona. "He's up here." Without waiting for an answer the man disappeared through the wooden swing door at the top.

She clambered up the wooden steps after him. Inside it was dark, since the large windows had been loosely covered with black-out cloth. She walked past the photo-litho machines and the piles of paper. Presses roared and clicked in the background and a couple of gawky apprentices stood staring at her as she followed the printer into a little room at the end of the printing shop.

It was hot inside. Electric heaters set in the roof burned bright red. Callum and Axel were seated on a pair of rickety chairs looking at some posters. Torn and crumpled paper littered the floor to ankle depth.

"They're good." Callum said. "They'll stand out well." Axel stood up as Fiona entered, pulled aside the black-out cloth and stared grimly out of the window. He made no attempt to greet her.

She picked up a chair and sat down facing the two men while the printer left to look after his offset presses. They started discussing among themselves in a vague ineffective way. Callum looked unhappy.

Fiona suddenly asked: "Why all this secrecy? Early on it was understandable. We couldn't let things get off to a half-hearted start. But now?" She was genuinely worried about the way things were being handled and had been for some time past. This had led to conflicts of loyalties which worried her. She had adopted the movement with a blind passion at first only matched by Axel's, but now the realities of bringing it into fruition allowed her glimpses of the problems to come. She looked anxiously across at them for their reaction.

"We still can't be sure of the result," Callum said.

"But for God's sake! We never will until we try for it," she burst out. "If it's going to succeed, then people must know and welcome it. This conspiring in the dark makes me, for one, feel uneasy."

"You know bloody well what to do if you don't like the way things are going." Axel shot her a hard look.

"Come off it, Axel. Don't be so touchy. Fiona didn't mean anything," Callum interjected.

"No?"

"I did indeed mean it," Fiona bridled. "It's been too hush-hush for too long. People will think we've got something to hide. Instead, we've got an open message to put across. We're trying to start a national, an international movement, remember?"

"So what?" Axel stood up and faced them, hands clenched by his sides. He kicked furiously at a sack of waste paper, and Fiona noticed that he was shaking. "So what?" he repeated. "You don't understand, you two. Most of the rest of the Committee are the same. It's not just us. It's not just a little student game. There's a bloody enemy and we're under attack.

Everywhere." He looked pointedly at Fiona. She blenched.

"And," he went on, "it's dangerous. There are to be no moves, no publicity until I . . ."

"You're not in charge, Callum is." She interrupted. It sounded petulant. Callum sat silently watching them.

"Neither of us is, damn it. We're only part of the set-up. We aren't Anarchists. You know that. We shouldn't aim for the headlines before we've written the small print. And then there's the money." Only with difficulty was Axel keeping himself under control.

"To hell with the money, and whoever of your secret friends is holding or twitching the purse-strings. Let the idea speak for itself . . . and soon." Fiona almost shouted the words. Her image of Axel as the scheming spider at the centre of his web flashed into her consciousness once again.

"I think that's enough from you. This thing is too important to be thrown off balance by a hysterical schoolgirl."

"Wait now. That's not necessary. Let's talk it over quietly." Callum's vague yet worried expression conveyed his perpetual concern to keep things peaceful.

"No, I'm sorry; I've kept quiet for long enough," Fiona went on. "Hysterical, maybe. But I can put it coolly enough on the record that I don't like the way things have been developing. We seem, we the whole Area Executive, seem to have lost any say in the business. Now all we do is sit around till Axel passes us the word from the 'sponsors', whoever they are, like Moses with the Tablets."

"That's about enough!" Axel was half smiling through his beard though his eyes were ice-cold. He had regained his efficient composure once again and her temper seemed to suit his purpose. His grin infuriated the girl. In desperation, she turned to Callum.

"Well?" she said. "You're meant to be in charge, aren't you?"

"Well, . . . I . . . er . . ." Callum looked helpless. He was out of his depth. They were both staring at him.

"I see." She looked away in contempt. "Then obviously it's

time for another National Council. We should put it to them to decide."

"*No*," Axel shouted. "No more damned meetings. It was founded democratically. That's enough. Now we have to take the decisions in this area, otherwise: anarchy."

"That's the second time you've mentioned anarchy. What you're suggesting sounds to me more like totalitarianism." She threw the words back at him. "That's my proposal. I'm sticking to it. Callum, I hope you'll act, do something. I'm going."

"That's fine by me." Axel said coldly. "Goodbye. Only remember one thing: keep your gossip to yourself. No running to anyone, Calder MacCaig for instance. You are still on the Area Executive, as you said, and gossiping, I can assure you, would only do us, you included, a lot, a great deal of harm. But then you wouldn't gossip would you? You're still loyal." He sneered at her.

"I'll do and speak to whom I choose." Bewildered, she glared back at him, aware that there had been a threat. His look, it was something uglier than she could remember seeing for a long time. There was real malice. She hadn't asked for anything like that. Then, tossing her long hair back from her face, she paced out of the room.

Callum sat with his head in his hands. What had happened? It was almost as if Axel had been provoking her. He waited for him to say something, to explain himself.

"You see the dangers? She's temperamental and could do a lot of harm if she were to talk. I'm afraid it won't do." Axel was staring blankly at a wall covered with old posters. He didn't really seem to be speaking to Callum, but more thinking aloud. As he did so, he pulled rhythmically at his beard.

"One's got to have discipline," he went on. "If she cracks, the consequences could be fatal. It could do a lot of harm at this juncture if things became public. People are already too interested in us, too interested."

Callum looked up and stared at Axel as if at a complete stranger.

Edinburgh, Sunday Evening

Walt Tesco was in luck. He had spotted his prey about five minutes before the announcement of the flight departure from Edinburgh, and had sidled up with a "Good evening, Minister. Tesco of the Federate Press Agency. We met after your speech to the Press Club about a month ago. You probably don't remember."

The Minister didn't remember, but gallantly lied about it. One up to Tesco. He had never met the Minister.

"Catching the London 'plane, Minister?"

They both were. Tesco slipped away to the ticket desk to try to change his Tourist-Class ticket for a First-Class seat. The Agency would probably pay the difference. If not, there were others who would. He had to wait what seemed like ages before the stewardess got round to him and the flight was boarding before he was issued with his new ticket. Then he had to rush to catch up with the other passengers, at the same time keeping his large untidy person a strategic and panting distance from his quarry, till they got into the aeroplane.

Tesco was one of the rapidly growing number of international gossip journalists, who followed their more acceptable news-gathering colleagues from disaster to scandal, lurking behind the main run of events in order to provide Europe's more sensational news-glossies with *human-interest* stories. Tesco was notorious for his inordinate ability to find the lower levels of gossip in quite innocent situations. But, as far as his employers were concerned, he had a knack of not quite ever pulling the story off, because of uncommon journalistic failings which included a certain kindness of heart when it came to writing about his victim.

On this trip Walt Tesco had taken a few days off, after covering the Lochinver by-election. It had been unrewarding stuff, most of it. The Lochinver Arms had been lousy, the food atrocious and the licensing hours unspeakable. He had regretted bitterly not taking up the scent of a new sex scandal in Cannes. But the past couple of days slumming it in Edinburgh had been enjoyable. It was remarkable what that fur-coated dour city could turn up if it tried.

Not that he had been idle. There had been this rumour he had picked up among the election gossip. Peculiar stories that didn't quite hang together. And the Minister's name had been involved in some way. Couldn't be better. What had the movement called itself?

Tesco kicked the elderly clergyman in the shin, and in the turmoil over apologising, managed, with quite a genuine-looking theatrical performance, to get his considerable bulk into his chosen seat beside the Minister.

An hour and ten minutes later as they landed at Heathrow, the Minister was promising himself that never again would he travel unprotected by his Private Secretary, Kent weekend or no Kent weekend. Not that he had given anything away to that tiresome fat slob of a journalist, with the funny middle-European accent and the halitosis. Nothing, that was, except his energy and his patience.

Walt Tesco, however, had come to the conclusion that there was something to hide.

SIX

Earls Court, Monday Evening

The pub was noisy and very crowded. The British always seemed to enjoy themselves in such surroundings, perhaps as a reaction to the coldness of their international reputation. Empty pubs were unpopular. Fill one, and it became yet fuller. The Victorian ceiling, rich brown with smoke, the painted wooden panels, the mirrors with ancient advertisements etched deep into the glass. The big breweries were re-creating places like this, but they could have this one for the asking, right down to the sawdust on the floor.

The drunk outnumbered the sober. Tension was heightening as "drinking-up time" approached. Mainly young art students and a few older men on the lookout for the easy young lays they had heard about; two or three ancients, cloth caps and shorts with their beer. One old man carefully emptied his whisky into a half of export.

The barman was brisk and brusque to the point of rudeness. No customer was right here. Take the place as you find it, or leave it. Self-selective, those who didn't like it, left. Those who stayed, fought their ways to the bar for a drink, then fought their ways back to corners to enjoy it, struggling to avoid spilling in the throng. Shout a conversation for a duration, then back to the bar for a refill. There were easier places.

The barman struck the big brass ship's bell. *M.S. Clarion.* Where and when had she sailed? Or had the bell been mass-produced for pubs.

"Time, Gentlemen, please."

The noise continued unabated, but there was a perceptible rush towards the bar for a last round. Axel looked at his watch, and pulled irritably at his beard. No contact. He'd have to telephone. They had promised this time, and he had wasted an evening. He could have used the time to do something about that little brunette who had been staring at him meaningfully for the past twenty minutes. Now some man in dark glasses seemed to have got her. Nice figure probably, under that yellow oilskin jacket. Fraction too much make-up, and God, the hair. Perhaps it was just as well.

Drunks everywhere. A nasty one pushing past him looking for the Gent's or, more likely, for a fight. One could tell the type. Axel stretched a casual foot out, almost without thinking, and the drunk crashed face downwards in the crowd. There was a female scream.

He moved away, pretending not to notice and headed for the door. Drinking time was up. There was a pull at the sleeve of his jersey.

"I saw that."

He spun round ready to defend himself. Then he smiled when he saw Stefan Issouna.

"You're late."

"Problems, Axel, you know how it is. I'm only over here for a flying visit and have so much to arrange and fit in."

"Let's go then. The pub is closing. We can talk in the street."

Outside, the drunk had found a fight. A sailor had been accused of having tripped him. The sailor was equally drunk, equally belligerent. There was the sound of a breaking bottle, a few shouts, someone laughing, and then, away in the distance, a police whistle.

"What's on?" asked Axel quietly, staring at the heavy face glistening in the lamp-light.

"They're getting too close, Axel."

"I've known that since Oslo."

"Yes, but the death of their man set them back quite a bit. Fortunately he didn't have the opportunity to pass on what he had discovered about my mission and my contacts here in London, but they know quite a bit about your team. We've got hold of a file and some papers as the result of assistance from another quarter. You're going to have to disappear, and soon. They know a great deal. They've even had a tail on some of you."

"But we're not ready." Axel mentally went through his carefully worked-out programme of action. There were several weeks of very hard work to be put in, quite apart from the extra fuss created by the impetuous Miss Fiona Ross and her demand for another National Council meeting. Things could get out of hand.

"I know you've problems, but you'll have to be ready. It'll have to do. Before you disappear, however, there are a couple of things outstanding. We must continue to humour the front men, but there are one or two danger spots that have to be ironed out."

Whitehall, Tuesday Morning

The ubiquitous Ministry of Works net curtains, supposedly camera-proof, were drawn tightly across the windows. The light from the grey London day wouldn't have been enough to illuminate the room even without them, and the big modern chandelier shone down brightly on the green felt on the conference table. The walls were lined with maps, and a blackboard and easel stood in one corner.

Eight or ten men, half of them looking like Civil Servants, the other half Civil Servants disguised as ordinary men. Each had a blotter, notepad, a carafe of water and a glass arranged precisely in front of him. In a large and ornate armchair at one end of the table, sat the Minister, one of a race apart, a political animal with his officials.

"To set the record straight at the start," the Minister began, "we've got to clear our minds. We're not just dealing with a bunch of students, idealistic, and so on. It's the infiltrators. We have the evidence. You know about the background to this so-called 'Norsemen' movement and I won't bore you repeating it. It's all in the Norslag File.

"We've had this sort of thing before: C.N.D.; Peace Movements; Vietnam Solidarity; and each time the idealists have walked, hand in hand, with the . . . er . . . others. Excuse the simplified division but you know what I mean. Maybe I'm not alone in this room in having protested and sat down outside this very building in Downing Street, or do public servants designate never . . ."

Polite chuckles ran round the table and a few people noisily lit their pipes. A joke had been made. The Minister paused shortly over his brief. He was aware it all sounded phoney, this hot-gospelling, now-I've-seen-the-light line, but he ploughed on:

"Here, however, we've something a bit worse. The Norsemen are internationally controlled. They're only a part of what in Scandinavia is, I believe, known as the Norslag organisation—that's a mongrelised name by the way, *norse* or northern, and *lag* which I'm told is Norwegian for a team or group. Whatever else, they're no amateurs. There has been one death so far, and this indicates that if they, whoever *they* are, are prepared to kill, then all this evidence about their getting at N.A.T.O. and our European policies generally, has to be taken very seriously indeed. And to make matters more difficult now, certain files on the Norsemen have been stolen. We are not quite sure that it was the result of unhappy chance; not quite sure," he repeated. "And it will demonstrate to you what we're up against for the future. You see one result." He gestured towards Rosetti, elegance somewhat restored, who sat at the far end of the table fingering the large piece of skin-coloured sticking-plaster on his forehead.

"I'm sure you'll join me in extending to Mr . . . er . . . er, in extending . . ." The words petered out in the general muttering of assent.

"The files," he went on, "as far as we have been able to establish, contained a very large part of what we know about the Norsemen organisation, including the latest political assessments. Fortunately the detailed Special Branch reports and other intelligence material were not held with the main papers in the Norslag File, so our work 'on the ground' so to speak has not been too drastically jeopardised. However, much of the information on the files could only have come from one or two people at the top of the organisation and a proposed contact we were going to plant . . . er . . . we were to have working for us, is now under suspicion from his potential colleagues. But because of his background he is still potentially extremely valuable to us, and we are trying to make him appear 'clean' and to arrange for him to attempt to persuade some of the more respectable members of the movement of the dangers they are exposed to. I need not burden you further with the details. But are there any questions so far? . . . Good. Then we'll continue. As to future operations, I have suggested . . ."

The Civil Servants listened, sitting back in their chairs or leaning forward intelligently on the green cloth of the table, each according to his habit. A few comforting pipes were re-lit. Some people took notes. At the far end of the table Rossetti produced a nail-file from his pocket and surreptitiously began to restore his battered fingernails to their former perfection.

Holborn, Tuesday Afternoon

Mrs. Rita O'Connell balanced her considerable form on the protesting chair. A wet cloth in one hand, a dry in the other, if she stretched, she could just reach to the top corners of the bow windows. She must ask Mr. McNab to get a brush. It was dangerous work. She had nightmares of slipping and going through the glass on top of all those old books. Mrs. O'Connell often had nightmares.

One . . . two . . . three . . . four. That was the top row dried and done. Why couldn't Mr. McNab get all those old panes done away with like the chemist next door had just done? So much easier to clean a big piece of glass. She had told him often enough. But he was stubborn, just like O'Connell himself had been. She stopped to rest and sigh, just as she always did over her memories. Memories were sweeter and more appealing than the reality had been.

Second row done, and the worst over. Third row to do and then she could get down off the chair. It was always the same.

Climbing down was getting more difficult though. Very inconvenient those panes. She had told Mr. McNab that he'd do better trade, especially with these students from the L.S.E. which was just a block or so away, if they could see in the shop window properly, see what he had to offer. He always answered back about atmosphere. But she knew in her heart of hearts that trade wouldn't ever be much better—even with a window like the new one in the chemist's next door. She always said the same to Mrs. McWhirter who sometimes came along to help her out.

Dusty, very dusty. No matter how hard she worked, and Mr. McNab knew only too well how hard that was, there was dust, so much dust everywhere. Mrs. O'Connell sighed heavily once again. At last the third row was clean. There was no doubt about that. It was so dark inside the shop that they reflected like mirrors. Better glass in row three. The top ones had been there since the year dot, so Mr. McNab used to say. They were old and the glass was warped. But the third row . . . She could see herself very clearly, and the narrow street behind her, almost deserted as it was early closing day.

She saw the two men in the doorway of the shop opposite. It had been a tailor's until the old man had died. Now it was empty. Perhaps they were buying? No, not them. Coat collars turned up, broad-brimmed hats well down. They reminded her of wartime gangster films. They'd be L.S.E. students probably. They wore the strangest clothes these days. Collars up like that! Not as if it was so very cold, even though it was the first of March. Quite warm really. No, it would be the new version of the maxi look, she decided. *New*. She laughed to herself. She had that photograph of herself with O'Connell on the beach. . . .

She gave a final polish to pane number four, row three, and began to think of her descent. Then she saw the girl's reflection. Scarf over her head, neat and tidy looking. The men appeared to step out of the doorway in front of her. There seemed to be some sort of struggle developing.

Mrs. O'Connell turned round to get a better look and immediately lost her balance. She fell heavily onto the pavement, but got to her feet again surprisingly quickly. She saw the men dragging the girl towards a car parked by the kerb. Student rag or no student rag, she couldn't stand hooliganism. Nor could O'Connell himself come to think of it. The girl was shouting and was obviously frightened.

Mrs. O'Connell picked up the bucket of water she had been using and hurried across the street. No one else seemed to be about. There were a few people much further down the street, but they were too far away to notice. Where was Mr. McNab? He was a bit frail, but he would have known what to do.

She had never done anything like it since the incendiary had landed on the stairs in 'forty-one. She threw the lot, bucket and water over them all. A wide-brimmed hat rolled in the gutter.

The men looked towards her in surprise for a moment and it gave the girl time to break free. They tried to follow but Mrs. O'Connell was in the way. They hesitated for a moment. One seemed to have a child's black toy pistol in his hand. He raised it, but the other man pulled him away. There was some shouting. The men jumped into the car, the engine roared into life, there was a screeching of gears, and it hurtled away along the street.

"Students! Now if they had been working lads like Mrs. McWhirter's Eddie, they'd have been arrested for that. Public nuisance. One law for the . . . How are you, dear?"

"A bit wet," said Fiona Ross.

"Sorry. The window water's a bit dirty too. Student friends? That it? Bit of skylarking?"

"Yes . . . Yes, that's it."

"I thought as much, though for a moment I thought it was for real. That toy gun—gave me quite a turn. A bit rough I'd say, dear. Choose your friends a bit more carefully in future. Like a cup of tea. Always welcome after a . . ."

"No, I . . . thank you. I must be going."

"Never mind. But your scarf's a bit untidy now. And do you want your friend's hat? Bit wet too, I'm afraid. Still, it serves him right, don't it."

"Yes it does, does indeed. Thank you ever so much. I must . . . go now." The girl was still staring in the direction the car had gone. She looked very pale.

"You sure you're all right, dearie. Easy done to put on a cup?"

"No. No thank you, really. I have to attend a lecture, and I'm late." The girl smiled fleetingly and then turned and walked rapidly away.

Mrs. O'Connell walked over and picked the empty bucket out of the gutter. She had mud on her dress from the fall. Nothing much. It would brush off.

Mr. McNab appeared at the doorway of the shop and called out: "Finished the windows yet, Mrs. O'Connell?"

"Nearly done, Mr. McNab," she shouted back. "Nearly finished."

SEVEN

Westminster, Tuesday Evening

"Tesco? . . . Tesco?" The Minister spoke enqu ringly into the green telephone.

"Says he did what? No, I don't think so. Oh yes, on the 'plane. That's right. Fat middle-European. Pebble-glasses? Yes, that's the chap. No, I told him nothing about . . . But come to think of it he did ply me quite heavily with questions, mainly concerned with the by-election result as I remember. I had got pretty thick-skinned about that by then as you'll appreciate, so I didn't really listen." As he spoke the Minister was drawing an elaborate doodle on the spotless blotter in front of him.

"Well if he knows a lot about it he didn't get it from me. No, I know you weren't accusing me. He's probably just speculating. . . . Yes, I see. But do you really think he's the sort of man to use? He seemed quite the opposite to me. . . . Of course it certainly would be good cover. No one in his senses would think we would employ . . . O.K. If you're so sure, then go ahead. I leave it to your discretion how to play this one. But it's important mind you, if only because the P.M. has it close to his heart."

The Minister placed the green receiver carefully back on the hand rest. His other hand still held the pencil which was completing the doodle. It was a stupid looking doodle. It had no character. He pulled the sheet of blotting paper clear of the leather writing pad and crumpling it up, threw it in the waste-paper basket. He had forgotten all about Tesco already. There were other more pleasurable things to occupy his mind. He reached across for the phone and got himself put through to a number in Mayfair. It rang for a few moments and then a woman's voice answered.

"Nicci? It's me," he said.

Lambeth, Wednesday Morning

They had kept entirely off the subject by unspoken mutual consent. Even sitting drinking together in the pub the night before, they hadn't touched on it. They had spoken about skiing, and MacCaig had talked, in so far as he was able, about what had happened in Iceland. Fiona listened mostly, wondering at the bitterness that had grown up in him since they last had met, trying to find out what he was like under the surface, what he really did for a living. She thought she had known him so well at University, but it all seemed so far away now, though it was only a few years. The gulf at times seemed too great between her research-student life, where freedom to plan her work and live as she wished was complete, and his employment somewhere in the fringes of the Establishment, where, she believed, he must lead a conformist, rigid existence, enclosed in endless files and bound with red tape.

But sometimes when she listened, the gap didn't seem to exist. Then she felt as close as before to this big angry man, who now walked with a limp. Perhaps it was this recently acquired injury which added to the attraction, calling out her instincts in a way which in other circumstances she would have thought ridiculously sentimental. She wasn't such a fool as to think he'd told her the whole story of how it had happened. Later, she had seen the scars on his body and knew with even more certainty that they couldn't have come from a simple fall on the ice. They were too thin and even.

They had laid together in bed, in his well furnished, if excessively neat, flat in a little square off the Kennington Road. In the light of the fire, she had watched him lying staring at the ceiling, talking in his soft West Highland voice. He always had seemed so robust and healthy, even after his convalescence, but tonight it wasn't just the half light that made him look drawn and tired.

She felt far from on top herself. It was only a few hours since the woman cleaning the windows had rescued her from . . . she wasn't quite sure from what. She hadn't even begun to think about it. She was still shocked and wondered if he noticed anything. She nearly told him about it, but held back, not wanting him to feel anxiety or pity. She would wait till later and then ask his advice. He would know what to do.

They made love. It was a surprisingly gentle business, but passionate for all that. She remembered the last time in his flat beside the University. It had been the same then. She lay back on the sheets, her head resting in the warm corner between his shoulder and chest. In a few moments, his regular breathing told her that he was asleep. She stretched cautiously not to disturb him, then she too relaxed.

Morning, and she woke up with a start with him standing over her fully dressed and holding two cups of Nescafé.

"I didn't hear you," she said, smiling shyly.

"I'm an early riser these days."

"When do you have to go?"

"I have to be in the Office in half an hour, but first I have to talk to you."

Her pleasure evaporated in an instant. She didn't want to talk. Why did men always have to spoil things, bring cold reality into something which should be warm and unspoken. She put the cup down and slipping out of bed, put his dressing gown on round her shoulders. She felt less vulnerable that way.

"Don't go. I will in a minute." His voice was quiet but the strange drawn look was back in his face, with something hard behind it. Only then she realised that it was something different.

It was a warning, he said. She must realise he meant it for the best. He wasn't speaking as an official but as a friend. She winced at the word, but sat very still on the edge of the bed.

He told her all about the Oslo business and the death there in the snow. When he saw the look in her eyes, he said that he had not believed it either. Now he did. He talked of infiltrators.

She didn't hear him out. He hadn't expected her to do so. He had no files filled with proof, no memories of a drunken Tinker to offer. She stood up, her eyes sparkling with anger. It was all lies, she said, or a deliberate act of provocation by the Establishment to which he belonged. The people she was with would have no part in such a thing. He had taken her off her guard when she was at her weakest, a sickening, underhand approach. He now should have the decency to go, or she would.

He was white as a sheet too. Having played it badly, he didn't try to explain further. He knew it would be hopeless and would sound like special pleading. He turned quickly and left the room.

It was only a few minutes later, as she stood alone in his flat, that the memory of the attackers of the previous day came back to her. She found her clothes in something like a panic and quickly dressed.

Soho, Wednesday Lunchtime

"Did you ever read a book called *Eminent Victorians*, Mr. Tesco?" Rossetti asked.

"No," lied Tesco, scowling slightly. He was on his guard against this man. What did he want? The only way was to play it along and find out.

All Tesco had done had been to ask for an interview with the Minister. He had got nowhere with that at first. The Head of the Ministry's News Department had coldly said he didn't think it was on, but he would ring back. He had. This time the man had been quite friendly. What was it again he had wanted to speak to the Minister about? Tesco had spilled a little to show what he knew, and to demonstrate that things couldn't be hushed up any longer.

"I'm afraid the Minister unfortunately isn't available," the urbane voice at the other end of the 'phone had said, "but if you'd like a bit of background briefing—off the record, you understand—and non-attributable, then come along at lunch-time on Wednesday."

Tesco had taken up the offer, and had been whisked off to lunch by this very unlikely host. All his instincts told him that something was amiss. Gossip journalists didn't get taken out to lunch—and at an expensive restaurant too—just for the colour of their eyes. This man Rossetti, or the Ministry he worked for, wanted something. Tesco had come across tactics like this before and was on his guard.

Rossetti was talking about Lytton Strachey—one of his idols apparently, and a very telling one at that. Most of what he said was rubbish. Tesco just happened to be well read on the subject, but decided to let the man prattle on. It would help get the man's measure, and he could debunk him later as required. Tesco might have a kind heart, but not when it came to pomposity. This offended him. It was dishonest.

But the Chateaubriand was excellent and the whole meal worth the boredom. And the service, so often lacking, Tesco found, even in the most expensive places in London, was polished and efficient. For Tesco admired efficiency in others as something totally unobtainable in his own disordered existence. He paused from his enjoyment of these material things to wonder when the point was going to come. To help things along, he interrupted Rossetti in the middle of some line about Strachey and Cardinal Manning, and with carefully studied, faulty English said, "I would about the Norsemen affair wish to know. Can you help me please?"

Rossetti stopped with a fork poised midway between his plate and his lips, as a whiff of slightly bad breath hit him.

"Oh, yes. Yes, quite. Yes, the Norsemen. But not so loud if you don't mind, Herr . . . Mr. Tesco. This is a confidential briefing. You did agree to that?—Strictly off the record, that sort of thing." Rossetti looked with scarcely concealed disgust at the sloppy ill-dressed figure sitting opposite him. What one had to do for the nation.

"We are worried, very worried." He bent forward towards Tesco in a conspiratorial fashion, ready to protect himself against any further odours.

"There is some evidence of infiltration. The movement itself is, er, no better or worse than many parties or movements, but on this occasion there are evil forces," he paused to underline the two words; *evil forces*, "at work."

"Why not expose them then?"

"Ah, we thought you might say that. But you see we can't just do it like that. There are influential sympathisers, some very important people, you understand. It's very difficult. We don't want to provoke a crisis, no warring sides so to speak. The P.M., I mean, *we* are anxious not to get hard and fast lines laid down."

"And so you want me to spread around a little gossip, that it?" Tesco's English had come rapidly back to its normal high perfection. "Then these important backers can withdraw before it's properly launched, without loss of face?"

"That's one possibility, Mr. Tesco."

"Whereas, if all this happened once it was launched, it would be much more difficult for them."

"I think you understand our position. Some more vegetables, Mr. Tesco."

"Thank you. The wine is very good."

"So sorry. Let me give you some more of that too."

"Thank you. O.K. Where do I start?"

"At the money side as always. Here are a few figures. You will see what a small percentage comes from overt backers and subscriptions. The rest . . . Perhaps you would like to see this report. I can give you a copy to take with you. You do read English well, I am sure, but you might like to memorise . . ."

"Yes, yes. I see what you mean." Tesco read avidly. The lunch had indeed been well worth it.

"Oh, and there is another little favour we would like of you."

"More, eh? You scratch my back I'll scratch . . ."

"If you like to put it that way, Mr. Tesco." Again the disgust was ill-concealed. "Yes, we are trying to . . . er . . . cast a little dissension in the . . . er . . . top management. Very delicate operation, you know what I mean."

"More dirt?"

Rossetti ignored the remark, and went on: ". . . and we would be grateful if you could get in touch with, or shall we call it interview, this person, a Miss Ross. She's on their Executive. While asking her a few questions, and from what we hear she may be less than responsive, just drop one or two of these figures and facts about the financial backing. Could you let us know her reaction?" It was like asking someone to organise a vicarage tea-party.

"Oh, and one last thing, Herr, I'm so sorry, *Mr.* Tesco. You realise that we have to have some . . . er . . . guarantees from you." Rossetti had kept the enjoyable bit to the end. It helped atone for him having to put up with the disagreeable lunch partner. "You get your story, and you help us. But you'll appreciate that we have to have a hundred per cent co-operation from you. No side-stories about our interest in all this, understand? Or I'm afraid it could be very unpleasant. You do have a British Passport, don't you? No—? That's what we thought. We hate having to take action in illegal immigration cases."

EIGHT

Earls Court, Wednesday Afternoon

Fiona ignored the bus queue and decided to walk. It wouldn't take her longer than twenty minutes to get to the Committee Rooms and it would give her time to think. She would go along and find the others, tell them what had happened and see what their reaction was. She shivered slightly and looked round nervously to see if she was being followed. Today she would keep to the busy streets, stay among the crowds. Nothing like that would happen to her again.

She had nearly dismissed it all as a dream or a case of mistaken identity, the attack outside the bookshop. That, or attempted rape or robbery. Perhaps Axel was right and she was getting too worked up about everything, dramatising an event that was . . . But it *didn't* fit. There was that gun. It had been no toy. The daughter of a soldier brought up in Malaya during the troubles knew a gun when she saw one. Then why hadn't she gone to the police? At first it had been the shock. Then, perhaps that old woman was right and it had been some student prank. She had decided to tell Calder everything, but that hadn't worked either. His inexplicable attitude this morning, which added to her confusion and uncertainty, kept coming back to her, no matter how hard she tried to dismiss both him and his story as pawns of the Establishment.

She found herself looking round again. Then she pulled herself together and coldly faced the reality that the attack must have been planned. She knew that now. But why? Was it to do with the Norsemen? Axel had said something about it not being a game—that there was a real enemy. Could it have been them, whoever they were?

She thought of Axel. For an instant an alarm sounded in the back of her brain. But it was all too preposterous. Admittedly, he had threatened her, and particularly about her contact with

Calder. Could he possibly have known that she was on her way to meet him last night? Could she really be important or dangerous enough in Axel's eyes for him to want to frighten her off or actually stop her meeting Calder MacCaig? It was surely too far-fetched and sounded more like the sort of story Calder had been trying on her that morning. And yet she had long had the opportunity of watching in close-up how Axel worked. It wasn't in his nature to leave things to chance, to accept people on trust, and in his eyes, indiscipline was the greatest crime of them all.

She looked round again. A fat, untidy-looking man, conceivably a tourist, wearing thick-lensed glasses and with a camera slung round his neck, was walking just behind her. He had been there when she had looked round before. His very untidiness made him stand out even in the crowded pavements. But she dismissed him. He looked too ridiculous for there to be any danger in that direction.

She looked at her watch. They would have started the Committee meeting by now. She would walk in as if nothing had happened at the last meeting in the printing shop, and would ask when the National Council was to meet. Axel could either accept or try to throw her off the Executive. And Axel still wasn't boss.

She stopped at the door of the house and pressed the bell. The electric catch buzzed and she pushed her way into the hall. She was so tense that she didn't notice that the door hadn't slammed behind her. Outside, Walt Tesco had bent down as if to fasten his shoe lace, and at the same time had slipped a folded newspaper in the door to stop it locking.

He waited outside for a moment until she had time to get clear. Then he too disappeared into the house.

The Committee were indeed sitting round the table already. She was obviously unexpected since the talking stopped as she came in. Without saying anything, she swept her long hair back from her face in a demonstration of her defiant unconcern, and took her usual place at the foot of the table.

"To continue," Axel said, without looking at her, "we have just heard from the Scandinavian Secretariat that things are well under way over there. But at the same time, they say that some of their colleagues have been arrested by the authorities, on what grounds we don't yet know." The others present looked suitably anxious. "We must expect the same to happen here," he went on. "For one reason or another we have them worried. They will try to cause dissension among us. They will try to find the weak links before we get fully launched. Time is of the essence." He paused for a moment and looked down at a letter in front of him.

"Two men tried to drag me into a car yesterday. One had a gun," Fiona interrupted quietly.

There were looks of amazement as she told them what had happened. Then Axel broke in rapidly: "Very interesting. But I don't believe you. Hysterical women aren't generally on the danger list. Probably a former lover." His eyes were hard as flint as he spoke.

Callum stood up as if to remonstrate, but just at that moment, Axel, who was sitting close to the door, jumped up and pulled it open. Tesco more or less fell into the room.

Axel grabbed him roughly by the jacket. "Who the hell are you?" he demanded. Everyone was standing now, the immediate tension of the scene with Fiona broken by this new interruption.

"I was looking for the Regency Stamp Auction. I was told it was here. This door was open." Tesco nervously adopted a thick accent once again. "Would you please release my jacket." He wheezed slightly as he tried to break free. Axel let him go at once and Tesco brushed limply at the crushed lapels of his suit, looking suitably injured as he did so.

"Sorry. We had burglars recently. My apologies for grabbing you like that, but one can't be too careful, and there is no company of that name here. This is a private house you see," Axel explained with surprising courtesy. "Will someone show this gentleman out."

"I'll go. But I'll be back," Fiona said. She recognised Tesco as the fat myopic tourist she had seen outside and she caught him looking at her now, but neither said anything. Now she would find out. At last a chance to get to grips with someone behind the mystery.

Half way down the stairs, she heard the door of the Committee room shutting. Then she turned to Tesco and said fiercely: "Who the hell are you and why are you following me? If you don't answer, I will scream, I promise you that."

"Don't worry, and please keep your voice down," came the anxious reply. "I was coming to see you, but a little later. . . . Name is Walt Tesco, journalist by profession. My entry into this house was purely fortuitous. I was going to wait till you had finished your meeting."

"What on earth are you talking about?"

"There's not much time or they'll wonder where you've gone, but let me say just this. Do you know where the money comes from?"

"What money?" Fiona was totally bewildered.

"Now my dear, don't be stupid. The money for your organisation of course. The lolly which your friend Axel produces. Let me give you this photostat of a bank transfer statement I have. Here, do you see? Can you read Cyrillic lettering?"

"Are you another plant?"

"It's my turn to ask you what you're talking about. I'm a simple journalist. Here's my card. You can ring me at this number any time."

They had reached the bottom of the stairs, and Tesco opened the front door.

"And one last thing, my dear. I heard you talking—you'll excuse my eavesdropping—about your accident yesterday. I'd be careful if I were you. My guess is that you needn't worry about it having been the authorities. They generally don't work that way, not mostly, anyway."

In a daze she walked back up the stairs clutching the piece of paper she had been given. Axel was standing at the top, looking down oddly at her. She gave a slight gasp when she saw him.

"The meeting's over for today," he said briefly. "We'll let you know about the next one." He turned and went back into the Committee Room and closed the door.

She was being ordered off. In her present frame of mind she wasn't prepared to argue, so she turned and walked slowly back down the stairs.

It was only afterwards that she realised she hadn't heard Axel open the Committee room door. He had been listening at the top of the stairs the whole time.

Whitehall, Wednesday Evening

"Quite *the* most revolting little man. I suppose I can't use the term 'little', 'gross' would be nearer to the truth. And his manners. I had to send my suit off to the cleaners at the first opportunity. He shared his food so liberally. Then his breath."

A nail-file was waved in the air to emphasise the point. "I cannot imagine why they should have chosen him. No one could ever accuse me of being insular or zenophobic, but his accent, and these dreadful pop-eyed glasses of his. Anyway, to cut a long story short, I was the chosen victim. I had ordered a very delightful little menu, and you know my taste in wine. Disastrous. All completely wasted. Thank goodness I can put in a claim for the bill, but not, unfortunately for the damage it did to my appetite.

"Anyway, at the end, I told him bluntly enough that he'd better be good, or we'd pull him in and throw away the key. He took it like a lamb. I think perhaps he expected as much. He knew he wasn't getting the story for nothing."

A theatrical look of pain appeared across Rossetti's face. He raised his hand to the piece of plaster on his forehead. It was now a week since his accident, but he felt the plaster rather suited him, gave him the slightly dashing appearance which he had always felt would best be set-off by a black eye-patch. There had never been the occasion.

His gesture went as unnoticed as his words. The solitary colleague left in the room had stayed late in order to get some work done and not to listen to other people's problems. Files were shuffled noisily about to indicate this. Rossetti on the other hand was staying late to report to the Minister. His tray was empty and time was hanging on his hands.

"If you ask me, I'm not sure at all how it's going to end. You know the Minister's reputation. This movement's ideas are not so far removed in spirit from some of the things he's said himself before now. And then there's the man MacCaig. D'you know him? He's the one who copped it in Iceland after that fiasco with the Communist submarines, and he's very bitter. I have heard it said that he's sailing a bit close to the ideological wind too. These security people of course. You can never tell which side they're on. Most of them are double-agents at the very least, and a close friend of his—I use the word advisedly—is this Miss Fiona What's-her-name on the Norsemen Executive. You know the woman. I sent that slob Tesco after her today, poor girl. I hear she's quite pretty."

"Damnation," he looked at his watch. "How long is this confounded man going to keep me hanging on. He wants to be kept closely in touch with everything, and then he spends half his time over at the House. How he expects people to have lives of their own, I just don't know."

Rossetti petulantly banged his empty filing tray down on the grey metal desk. His colleague looked up startled and annoyed. "What the devil's the matter? Can't you relax. I have work . . ."

"Sorry, sorry. I thought you'd be interested. It's got its international implications too, you know. The Swedes and the Norwegians have pulled in one or two of the top people. We're under pressure to do the same, but the Minister is biding his time. I can quite believe that . . . Oh, are you going? I thought you were staying late to get some work in. Oh, goodnight then."

The door slammed and Rossetti was left alone musing at the temperamental nature of some of his colleagues. Sometimes they were very difficult. He smiled resignedly to himself.

Oslo, Wednesday Night

"This direct dialling system is all right when it works, but that's not often, especially in international calls. That's the tenth time I've dialled London," Schoeyen said nervously. He hated his guest.

"Get on with it, and let me know when you're through. It's urgent. I've been waiting long enough."

Stefan Issouna dabbed at his forehead with a clean silk handkerchief. He walked impatiently through into the living-room and up to the big picture window. It was a bright night, and beautifully clear. The moonlight hit the thin line of the fjord in the distance. Inside, it was hot. He had turned the central heating up again, damn him.

He went through and seized the telephone.

"Hello, Axel. That's right it's me, Stefan. Now listen carefully. I want you over here as soon as you can make it. I'm calling in everyone for consultations. Since I saw you in London two days ago, I've had dozens of reports. They are clamping down hard, though so far they've picked up the wrong people. But they're worried. The . . . er . . . accident here, as I told you, lost them a lot of information, and the papers we got our hands on were extremely valuable, so we've gained a few days. . . . Yes, yes, I appreciate you have your problems. We should have given you some more assistance earlier. O.K. if you can deal with that particular problem very quickly I can give you a week, but no more. That would mean you could be here next Wednesday, Thursday morning at the latest. We'll have started, but I'll bring you up to date when you arrive. . . . What's that? A journalist, yes. I see. Well he's obviously a plant. But in a way if the story breaks it's no bad thing, so long as they don't try to discredit us further for the time being. . . . O.K. We'll send some help, and you know who to call on, but there isn't much time. You must ensure that your Area Executive don't do anything foolish while you're away. Can you guarantee that? Hello? Hello? Hell . . . and Damnation. The line's gone."

"Shall I try to get through again?" Schoeyen looked worried.

He feared the prospect of yet another outburst from Stefan Issouna.

"No matter. He got the message. But one thing to oblige. Could the central heating . . .?"

"Certainly. At once."

NINE

Pall Mall, Thursday Night

The Minister could identify the precise moment very early on in his career when it had dawned on him that his private life had almost gone and his public life had taken over. He had been wandering in Soho late one evening after an official dinner, and, fortified by the wine and the brandy, was loitering guiltily on the threshold of a strip-club. Sufficiently persuaded of his anonymity, he had made up his mind to go in, when he heard his name called, and a group of his most puritanical constituents had borne down on him. Sweating heavily, he had explained his presence perhaps a shade too hastily, but fortunately they were full of the conference they were attending in the big city, so no great harm was done. He had expansively invited them all to lunch at the House the next day as self-inflicted punishment, not for having almost lapsed, but for almost having been found out. Since then, his lapses had been well-concealed, in the knowledge that privacy and public office are poor bed-fellows.

For the earlier part of the evening at least, there was not exactly a scruffy liaison to hide. Had there been, he would have chosen his Club. But it was here, rather than at the Office or at the House, that he had chosen to meet MacCaig, free from note-taking officials and over-attentive private secretaries.

They had given him MacCaig's confidential report, and he had been more than a little intrigued by the picture it gave of the agent who had been chosen to try to break the Norsemen. The doubts and political emotions showed through clearly, yet the Establishment had cleverly managed to persuade him. It was the doubts and emotions that were fascinating as some sort of attraction of likes. It had been so similar when he himself had been persuaded by the Prime Minister. The Establishment won in the end, usually.

So he had selected his Club rather than the Office. They had never met and it might be easier to meet on more neutral territory. Easier for what? He wasn't quite sure how things would turn out. Was this unknown man to be the foil he was looking for or the opportunity to talk to someone who might understand?

The big marbled hall was empty except for the one-armed porter. As always, the electric light seemed too weak to do its job and the place was gloomy and cheerless, helped on by the decaying leather armchairs, the faded etchings on the walls, and a modern hideous wallpaper, the result of a House Committee's attempt to produce a more swinging atmosphere in what otherwise was a miserable tomb. A fairly typical upper-class London Club.

MacCaig hadn't arrived yet and so the Minister made for the bar, leaving a message for his guest. To have waited would have added to the unusual circumstance of a Minister asking a relatively junior and unknown official to dinner.

The place was almost deserted. A few old members sat reading by the big open fire. Two young ones perched on stools by the bar were talking too loudly for the surroundings. He picked up a late edition of the *Evening Standard* from a table and went and sat in a corner.

"Something to drink, Minister?" A dyed-blonde barmaid of wartime vintage, who had taken on traces of the faded though expensive shabbiness of the place, hovered above him. He ordered a whisky and turned to the front page. The main headline was about the car workers' strike, but there were a couple of column inches at the foot of the page, datelined Munich, referring to a report in a German illustrated weekly about potential political scandals in Britain. It mentioned the Norsemen and some talk about its funds, but there was no comment.

It was a typical interest-whetting piece. Tesco had done his stuff and it had been picked up. The editor of the *Standard* hadn't committed himself to anything, but despite the briefness, plenty of people would notice it. It would build up dangerously.

"Good evening, Minister." A tall, slightly stooping, dark-haired man was standing over him.

"Ah, you're MacCaig. Sit down. Have a drink." The barmaid, a single glass on her tray, was standing behind the new arrival.

"Whisky? Good. That's the stuff." The Minister was talking jovially in an attempt to create an informal atmosphere. He stopped when he saw it wasn't going to work.

"We've met somewhere before?"

"A long time ago, Minister. Relatively, that is. University. Union debates. You perhaps remember one where a bucket of paint was introduced into the argument?"

"Wait . . . yes. Weren't you with the . . ."

"Yes, I was an ardent Nat' then. I still have inclinations." They both laughed.

"I know, I know." Things began to fit conveniently together in the Minister's mind. It promised to have been a wise invitation after all, and it wouldn't necessitate much delving into backgrounds. MacCaig was already neatly pigeonholed.

The two men sat back in silence with their glasses of whisky. The young club members by the bar were still talking loudly. One was on about his conquest of the previous night.

"I suppose you are wondering why I suggested this meeting?" The Minister tried hard not to sound too pompous.

"That's true."

"To be quite honest then," he lowered his voice, "I wanted to keep this whole business under control. The only way to do that is—with apologies for the expression—to know your man. Personal files are one thing, personal contacts are another."

The guest looked almost hostilely unconvinced, and the Minister realised that he would have to change his tactics. It was going to be difficult.

"When do you leave for Oslo?"

"It depends when the story breaks."

"It has. It's in the late edition of the *Standard*. That man Tesco's done his work. Here." He handed the newspaper over.

"Then I'm off within twenty-four hours, I expect."

"And you are happy about that?"

"You'll have read it all in my file, Minister. You know my feelings. I hope we can avoid going through it all again." MacCaig's voice was stony.

"Oh don't worry. I'm not going to subject you to another inquisition. Far from it. You know my background too. You'll understand when I say that I almost sympathise."

"I've heard it suggested."

". . . sympathise with you, I mean. I have no time for the way these people have gone about things."

"It depends which ones you're talking about."

"Of course. The goodies and the baddies. I suppose it's generally known that I was reluctant to take this thing on?"

"Yes."

"And does rumour tell you why I did in the end?"

MacCaig was silent.

"I'll tell you why. My hand was forced. You probably know. But now I don't care nor regret it for a moment. These people are evil."

"My own view too, Minister," MacCaig replied woodenly. He hoped this confessional wouldn't go on too much longer.

"And you're wondering why I'm telling you all this? But your glass is empty. Another? . . . No? Then shall we go through for dinner?"

Some two unsuccessful hours later and a mile away in one of the less respectable of Mayfair's streets, the Minister pressed one of a row of doorbells outside a white-painted Victorian block of flats. The intercom by the bells crackled a question, the Minister bent and muttered a word of introduction and the electric lock on the oak door buzzed open. He pushed his way into the familiar, red-carpeted hall.

That morning he had passed on a message to his wife saying that he was sorry but urgent Government business once again would prevent him from coming home on the night flight as he had promised to do that evening. He hadn't spoken to her himself. One of his secretaries had telephoned. He couldn't have tolerated the inevitable row on top of everything else.

As he went up in the lift he suffered his usual brief bout of guilt. His wife would be in bed by now. Tomorrow she would carry out the odd constituency engagement on his behalf and would do it well. Meanwhile he was in Mayfair tensely looking forward to the pleasures to come. But as always, he shut his conscience with a snap as the lift stopped automatically on the fifth floor. Nicci was waiting for him.

He had first met her at a cocktail party given by a mutual friend in his Dolphin Square flat. He had, as usual, been on his own, and she, the sparkling young wife of a slightly decaying Opposition M.P., was also alone, her husband away on a Parliamentary fact-finding tour of South East Asia. He had homed on her at once and using the nodding acquaintance he had with her husband as sufficient pretext had introduced himself to her. With her long fair hair and a provocative figure which her almost translucent dress did little to disguise, he found her immediately spellbinding. She responded warmly, with an ease that made him quiver with anticipation, and to say the least, their relationship had blossomed quickly. They didn't actually sleep together that first night, but the fact-finding tour of South East Asia was a lengthy one and the call of his official duties far from pressing at the time, so the opportunity over the following weeks was extensive. He, attracted by her intellect but more by her remarkable sensuality, and she, driven by a combination of childlessness, her deep dissatisfaction with an ever more alcoholic and ever less promising spouse, and by a genuine and constant sexual starvation, would have been inevitably drawn together even if the immediate opportunity had been lacking.

Even after his colleague's return from South East Asia, their meetings managed to be both frequent and discreet. The Minister considered his bachelor flat too squalid a rendezvous for their highly polished infidelity, and she had a curious access to a friend's flat in Mayfair, where they met at least once a week during her husband's absence in his constituency. For she, unlike the Minister's own wife, insisted on her right to remain permanently in London, arguing that her own life was more important that nurturing her husband's constituency. It was only infrequently and just before elections that she dragged herself away to sit loyally on platforms at political meetings and to open village flower shows.

But the Minister had no illusions that the sexual and other demands of this vivacious woman were or could be satisfied permanently by him alone. From the start, therefore, they had an unspoken agreement that they would live only for the present in their relationship, both of them knowing that she was a bird of passage, who one day would move on with only the slightest intimation that the affair was at an end.

Tonight she was wearing the tight black-leather dress that he had especially admired. Her fair hair hung loose over her shoulders, and round her neck, a simple silver pendant hung by a chain, gently caressing the cleft exposed by her low-cut neckline.

The flat was warm and inviting. Two crystal glasses, a jar of ice and a bottle of Johnnie Walker Black Label stood on the low coffee table by the marble fireplace. The pure white bear-skin rug he had bought her was rumpled and in the middle lay an open book of short stories. She had been lying there reading and waiting for him. It seemed all so perfect, and yet when he came in he at once sensed something different in her behaviour.

They didn't say much, for that evening there was little either of them wanted to say. He was preoccupied by his own worries and by his awareness that something new had entered her life, something that had come between them. What it was didn't really matter. Perhaps it was another man, perhaps she had simply tired of him, but he knew then that the peak had passed, that it would be pointless to try to prolong it, that it was the beginning of the end of the affair. And the detail didn't matter much.

So they sat opposite each other in the two deep chairs by the fire. She spoke little and he volunteered nothing. Nor did he probe into the new thing in her life nor question the future of their relationship. That had been part of the bargain from the beginning. Yet for a moment he felt like pouring it all out, telling her he wanted it otherwise, that he needed her permanently, but he knew that it would precipitate the end and that, in any case, it wasn't true.

She poured him a drink, while he sat quietly watching and waiting, realising that as always she would want to do things in her own time. After a while they came automatically together, but their embrace was an empty one. Then lust took over, when she deliberately reached across to him and led his hand to where her silver pendant gently dangled.

After only an hour he left. He excused himself to her saying that he had to get up very early the next morning. He realised that she knew he was lying. But he went because he did not wish to face a second let down that evening and because he felt he might salvage some pride by taking an initiative in the parting. He hoped she would press him to stay, to spend the night as he had wanted. But in the event she didn't press him and their parting was a lifeless formality.

Lambeth, Friday Afternoon

Swallowing her pride, Fiona went to see him, to tell him, to get it all off her chest. She was frightened and despite their row she knew she could rely on him, whereas there was no saying what that fat little man Tesco could provide in the way of help, despite his offer to her to ring him anytime. She had thrown away the piece of paper Tesco had given her, believing it was a further plant. Now she just didn't know what to believe. She felt desperately alone; her support for the Norsemen still was there but, for the moment, it was buried under the weight of her own experiences. She had tried Callum too, but he had been at his most vague and uninvolved, when she went to see him, so that she had given up almost at once and had left in exasperation and despair.

There was no reply when she rang the doorbell of his flat. Her heart sank and she was about to leave when a door on the same landing opened and a woman in curlers stuck her head out.

"You want Mr. MacCaig?"

"Please."

"'fraid he's went away. For some time, he said. I've cancelled the milk for him. Gone abroad."

Fiona started to go back down the common stairs, but the woman called her back.

"You ain't a Miss Ross by any chance?"

"Yes . . . but." Fiona stopped, puzzled.

"I'd forgot. There's a letter for you. Sorry. Mr. MacCaig said there was a hundred-to-one chance you might appear. I'll just get it."

It was to the point: "I'm glad you've come," it read, ". . . but anxious because it means the heat is on. Perhaps you realise now how serious it all is. I don't mean to preach. Sorry not to be available, but if you feel there's any immediate danger or if you'd like to help, ring my office without delay. It's very important. Just give your name. It will be familiar to them, I'm afraid.

"You probably won't do that and I'll quite understand. But in that case, for God's sake lie low for a bit. They think you're going to spill the beans to me and they may try to stop you. Go up to Scotland to my aunt and uncle, for example. They'll remember you and you'll be welcome."

Whitehall, Friday Evening

Rossetti came into the office without knocking, strode across the worn carpet and banged the metal-lined despatch box down heavily on MacCaig's desk. The latter looked up irritably from inspecting his air ticket to Oslo.

"You're MacCaig? How do you do. Pleased to . . ." The visitor extended a well-manicured hand and had it ignored.

"Who let you in here? Don't you realise this is a security zone?" MacCaig remarked angrily without getting out of his chair.

"Don't get all worked up. I have a pass and it's you I've come to see."

"No time. Sorry. Come back in a couple of weeks. I have a plane to catch and I'm just leaving. And take your despatch box off my passport, will you." He scowled ungraciously.

"My goodness. . . . Hardly polite. But never mind. I'm afraid I have to disappoint you. I've just caught you in time. Papers here for you. Most urgent and to do with your trip." Rossetti nervously jangled a chain of keys and eventually managed to find one that fitted the box. He opened it and passed MacCaig a red folder.

MacCaig snatched it impatiently from his hands, opened it and began to read.

"So you see your trip's off for the time being. Looks as if you've got quite a problem on your hands. If I can suggest . . ."

MacCaig looked rudely up and said "Hush" in a loud voice. Rossetti lapsed into wounded silence.

The main paper in the folder was the monitored transcript of the telephone call between Axel in London and an unknown man about a meeting in Oslo the following week. So Axel was the link man after all. The day Calder's employers had persuaded him to take on the Norsemen business, when they had told him about Tinker's death in the snow, he had read about the official suspicions of Axel's crucial role, but he hadn't been convinced. After all, he had known Axel on and off for years, ever since University.

He turned to read a covering report which noted that as a result of the conversation, Axel had booked a flight to Oslo for that evening. Glancing at his own ticket MacCaig realised that they were to have been on the same plane. That would have spelled its own dangers since Axel would notice him at once and would put two and two together. As the Oslo meeting wasn't till the following week, Axel must have tidied up the problems he had been worried about when he spoke on the telephone, and much quicker than he had expected. MacCaig wondered why.

A further document from the security people in Oslo gave

some background to the meeting, where and when it was to be held. The international organisers behind the operation had been getting pretty jumpy as a result of the arrests and this was to plan the next stage. It was a council of war.

The third paper was a brief instruction to postpone the trip pending further developments. MacCaig muttered under his breath but he saw the force of the argument. With Axel over there, he could hardly be expected to pick up any of the threads dropped by Tinker, particularly as the Norweigan security people weren't apparently too keen to arrange for any more special investigations until the murder of Tinker had been cleared up. And with Axel on the spot to identify him, MacCaig would stick out like a sore thumb. There was certainly some rethinking to be done.

MacCaig considered the possibility of setting a tail on Axel, but he discarded the idea at once as being unlikely to pay dividends even if Axel didn't spot that he was being followed more or less straight away. He would probably be expecting some such action by the authorities. It would have to be more direct and final a move if it were to be successful. One minor detail had caught MacCaig's eye. The telephone conversation had been interrupted before the end. Supposing, just supposing Axel had wanted to say something more, make some emergency plan about sending a relief if anything misfired and he was unable to attend himself. If Axel were forcibly prevented from going to Oslo, what about someone taking his place, like, like Fiona Ross? And Axel wasn't expected in Oslo for another five days so there was time to lay the operation on. MacCaig glanced at his watch and then looked across at Rossetti who had been kicking his heels impatiently in a corner of the office.

"Would you like to make yourself useful?" he asked, a fraction less arrogantly.

"You put things so nicely," Rossetti muttered sulkily.

"Find out where the girl, Fiona Ross, is."

"I, we know."

"Where?"

"She was at your flat this afternoon, picked up a letter

you left for her and then went off. You should know that."

"Damnation." MacCaig had forgotten his helpful advice in the rush of preparing for his Oslo trip. "And now where is she, since you're so clever?"

"On her way north on the night train. We've been following her this end for several days, and our people up there will carry on the tailing when she arrives. You do know by the way that someone tried to kidnap her in the open street last Tuesday?"

"But that was the day I met . . ." MacCaig was taken off his guard. It suddenly dawned on him that quite a number of people knew where Fiona had spent Tuesday night.

"Precisely." Rossetti looked knowing and then smiled primly. "And so she didn't tell you, otherwise you would have told us, wouldn't you?"

MacCaig resisted the strong temptation to wipe the smile off the visitor's face. Instead he said: "Bugger off."

"I beg your pardon?"

"You heard. And as you go, get this air ticket cancelled. I may need a flight again next week, though—two flights. Oh, and I need a taxi straight away to take me to the airport. Call me one, will you?"

"Who do you think you're talking to?"

"I've not the faintest idea. Maybe your mummy can tell me. Now run along. There's not much time."

TEN

Heathrow, Friday Evening

A work-to-rule among ground staff had led to some flights being delayed and the International Departures lounge was crowded. But there was still a half hour till the scheduled take-off for Oslo and the flight had not been called. The air was full of the cries of tired children and the irritated or consoling voices of their parents. The labour dispute had spread to the canteen staff as was obvious from the filthy floors littered with paper cups and other refuse. An elegant middle-aged woman, in a wide fur coat, brushed past a plastic-topped table over-loaded with empty beer bottles and glasses, and a few were knocked to the ground. She walked on unaware, and the jagged pieces of glass lay unattended where they fell, gradually being crushed and splintered among the other rubbish.

MacCaig walked slowly through the throng searching for Axel. If they could pick him up before the passengers started boarding, it would save having a scene and arresting him in the middle of a lot of other people. The airport police were alerted and a Special Branch man was keeping a few discreet paces away. He kept well in to one side of the lounge, expertly scanning the crowd, conscious always of the unusual heavy weight hanging by his left shoulder, where a gun nestled in its holster. He had been reluctant to carry one, since he knew he would be working in a crowded and confined space, but in the end, and remembering Tinker, he had persuaded himself of the painful necessity. He paused briefly by the information desk where harassed air hostesses were trying to pacify delayed, angry passengers. He turned slowly, re-checking that he hadn't missed Axel in the part of the lounge he had already surveyed. As he did so, his hand came up automatically once again to feel the reassuring bulge under his left arm.

The plan was simple: pick up and hold Axel and persuade

Fiona to take his place later. The first part was easy; MacCaig wasn't too happy about the second. It wouldn't be easy to persuade Fiona, quite apart from getting her accepted by the people at the Oslo meeting. They could be far from sure that she wasn't already highly suspect and a most unlikely substitute for Axel. Still it would, with luck, gain them access to the people behind the conspiracy. They would be unprepared.

A Rome flight was called and beyond the rush of people making their way to the gates, MacCaig suddenly saw Axel standing by the bookstall thumbing through a copy of *Playboy*. He walked slowly towards him signalling cautiously to the S.B. man that he had spotted him. The airport police were nowhere to be seen, but they were efficient, knew how to handle things and would be particularly alert since they had been told that Axel was a suspected hi-jacker. That was enough. He might be armed and there could well be a struggle since he would know at once what MacCaig's presence meant for him.

Perhaps Axel saw the reflection in the glass window of the bookstand, perhaps it was some sixth sense, but when he turned round, it was suddenly, and he already held a gun in his hand. An American woman with a small child in tow, who was buying some picture postcards, dropped her bag with a scream and tried to grab at her child. But Axel had already pulled the startled boy in front of him as a hostage, and was edging towards a nearby exit. The child let out a piercing yell of fear, and MacCaig and the Special Branch man stopped helplessly in their tracks. Passengers milled around them, most of them unconscious of the drama that was being played out. One elderly man seeing that something was amiss, went up and started to remonstrate with Axel for making the child scream, and was sent flying across the floor for his pains. By this time several other women had joined the child's mother in her hysteria and there were shouts of "Madman", and "Look out, he's got a gun." Someone laughed and said it must be a film, but then everyone became alert all at once and a great part of the departure hall cleared as if by magic.

Axel reached the exit and began to back through it, still

facing MacCaig, still holding the now hysterical child in front of him as a shield. At that moment a young airline steward appeared in the doorway behind Axel. Perhaps he hadn't seen the gun, but ignorance was no help. A shot rang out and the steward crumpled up where he stood. The swinging exit door banged sickeningly against the writhing body and Axel had disappeared. The little boy was still there, however, abandoned and now pale and silent.

It had all happened so quickly. Only a few seconds had passed and several people rushed forward to help. MacCaig was already through the door, the Special Branch man close behind him. They jumped over the inert body of the steward as they went. Others would look after him.

The exit led to a small customs examination room, empty except for a few suitcases. A second door at the far side banged shut as they entered. The two men ran across and swung through it to be faced with lift gates leading to the underground parking area. The lights above the gates indicated the progressive descent of the lift to the bottom. Axel had been lucky to find it ready and waiting.

"There's a fire escape just round the corner," shouted the S.B. man, and together they raced towards it and down the metal steps to the parking lot.

It was dark below, after the glaring neon of the departure lounge, and cars were parked tightly round the thick concrete pillars which supported the roof. They stopped, adjusting their eyes to the gloom. There was no sign of Axel. A handful of people were wandering about, getting in or out of their cars, and a white-coated attendant was directing new arrivals in a loud complaining voice. The S.B. man went up and questioned the man who obviously thought it was a joke, and started to become abusive. The policeman produced his identity card and the man became slightly more helpful. No, he hadn't seen anyone.

At the far end of the area a motor car engine roared into life and a little Volkswagen hurtled round a row of cars towards them.

"Look out, it's him," MacCaig shouted, leaping back into the cover of a pillar. The shout was drowned by the noise of the engine and the Special Branch man turned too late. The car hit him but didn't stop. Axel, seated in the driver's seat, crouched forward over the wheel, staring fiercely in front of him. He drove straight towards the red and white painted barrier at the exit and, without decelerating, crashed through, shattering the windscreen in the process. MacCaig ran futilely after it as it careened, tyres screaming, up the narrow track to the road.

As luck would have it, an empty taxi was partially blocking the entrance. Axel didn't brake. Perhaps he couldn't see properly through the shattered windscreen or perhaps the brakes failed. Whatever, MacCaig knew he didn't need to run any more, from the way the car door burst open and the driver's body was thrown out on to the roadway. It rolled over several times like a limp rag doll, and lay still against a "No Parking" sign by the kerb.

Fleet Street, Friday Night

Walt Tesco just happened to be sitting on the edge of the sub-editor's desk when the agency tape was brought in. He barely gave it a glance at first. Would-be hijackers killing themselves were hardly in his line of interest. But a few minutes later when the photo-service brought in some rough proofs, his attention was caught by something vaguely familiar.

"Who took these?" he asked sharply.

The sub turned towards Tesco and yawned openly. "Hang on a minute. Let me finish this story," he said glumly.

The room was stuffy and smoke-filled as always by that time of night, but as the central heating wasn't too effective, no one actually dared to open the window and let in the cold. There was already too much noise filtering through the glass from the street below, as the lorries brought in their new supplies of newsprint and the yellow delivery vans prepared to rush off with the early editions.

The sub bent over his copy. Tesco knew it would be pointless trying to rush the man. It was getting near the deadline and he still had a lot to cover. There was another Middle East crisis getting into full swing and the agency tapes were full of material to be digested and edited. He had already made it clear that he could have done without Tesco hanging about gossiping, as well, and he was scarcely civil.

Eventually he put down the copy he was working on and reluctantly took time to tell Tesco that it was one of the hack photographers at the airport, someone who usually only dealt with journeying film stars. He had been right on the spot.

Tesco remembered the man and with some difficulty got him on a line.

"These photographs. . . . First class. No, I don't know if they're going to be used, but I've got a different angle which may be worth something to you. Did you send in to us all the ones you took?"

"No," the photographer replied. "As usual I only printed the higher quality ones."

"Any of the face?"

"What face?"

"The hi-jacker's, of course. Close-ups."

"It wasn't very nice in close-up, though the man's beard covered up some of the mess, but I may have something."

"Get it over here straight away. If my theory's correct, you've just earned yourself an extra ten quid."

"Thanks very much, Mr. Tesco. Anytime."

An hour and a half later, Tesco was sitting with a magnifying glass in one hand, a pile of glossy prints on the desk in front of him. Through the blown-up grain and despite the blood, there was no doubt about it. It was the man they called Axel, the bearded man who had grabbed him and then politely shown him out of the Norsemen meeting, the man who, he had been told, was the channel for the funds.

Tesco thumbed through the prints slowly. So Axel was dead, killed while attempting to hi-jack. Somehow Tesco didn't think that could possibly be it. Once again, the Norsemen business had taken on a new lease of life.

Argyllshire, Sunday Afternoon

Away below, a small motor boat rode heavily at anchor to the lee of the little island. Gulls wheeled dramatically from the cliff top in mad plunges at the waves. The bitter north-east wind whipped the heather into a wild accompanying dance and the ominous charcoal-grey clouds swept invincibly towards the blurred horizon. Only the rocks stood still, dark and glistening after the recent downpour. Fiona, sheepskin coat lightly around her against the blast, stood and watched unseeingly.

She had run away. Now a mixture of guilt and anxiety had settled on her, guilt that, after months of planning the Norsemen, she had run out on the others just when the whole thing was set for launching; anxiety that she should have given in to an escapist whim as the result of a series of probably disconnected incidents. Calder's letter had given the final push, and now she regretted it. At this distance it was all so unreal and ridiculous.

She would tell Calder's aunt and uncle that she was going straight back on Monday's boat. They were kind and understanding, and would accept this with the same unquestioning grace as they had welcomed her. She would go back and carry on as though nothing had happened. They needed her help. Even Axel would appreciate her return, especially if she avoided ridiculous dramatics and an over-questioning curiosity in future. The others knew what they were doing and who was she to question it when the only thing that really mattered was the success of the movement. She had behaved foolishly. Meanwhile the island air was invigorating after London and she would make the most of it.

A path led down the face of the cliff, at times cut into the sheer rock, and she began to scramble down it towards the shore. It was almost deserted. Over to the west where the island sloped more gently to the sea, she could see a farmer on his tractor at the spring ploughing. It moved slowly across the field followed by a huge cloud of sea birds. The tide was high and the little motor boat had weighed anchor and was now drawn up close to the sand. Two men in oilskins standing beside it looked up towards her as she made her descent. A third figure was sitting in the stern of the boat, his hand resting on the tiller.

A rabbit darted across the track in front of her, startling her, and she almost lost her footing, so from then on she went very carefully and seldom took her eyes from the path. By the time she reached the bottom, the two men had left the boat and were waiting for her. She looked up at them enquiringly.

"Excuse me. Fishing and run out of diesel. Can you tell us where we can buy some about here?" one of the men explained shortly. He was wearing a suit of oilskins many sizes too big for him, and on his feet an incongruous pair of black patent shoes.

"Perhaps the village store," she answered. They didn't look like fisherman. Pale, somehow familiar-looking city faces, and it was an odd time for holidaymakers.

"Can you tell us how to get there?"

"Go along the shore, beyond that farm over there, then you'll find the road. It will take you about twenty minutes to walk, I'm afraid . . . I'm going part of the way. I'll show you," she added helpfully.

They walked back down in the direction of the boat in silence, and she started to lead them along the shore in the direction of the village. She didn't pay much more attention to them and she certainly didn't feel like chatting. They weren't particularly her type and she had plenty of her own thoughts to occupy her.

Then one of the men spoke out sharply. He was only a couple of paces behind her: "That's far enough. Keep on to the boat, Miss Ross."

At first she thought she had misheard. She turned round and the questioning smile faded from her face. One of the men had a gun hidden in a fold of his oilskin. Only now she recognised him as one of her attackers from the previous week. She gasped and instinctively tried to move away.

"What? Is this some kind of game?"

"You heard. The boat, and quickly. There's not much time." The man's voice was hard.

"Who are you? How do you know my name?" She knew the answer as she spoke. Her heart was beating wildly.

"No questions. The boat, I said."

Reluctantly she did as she was ordered, at the same time looking round for any possible help. Still the only other person in sight was the ploughman, several hundred yards away. It would be useless to shout against the wind.

She was made to scramble aboard the motor boat as best she could. The two men followed after her, with some difficulty pushing it off the sand as they came. They were obviously unused to boats. On board, they sat facing each other on a circle of lockers set round the cockpit. The engine was already running and the bows immediately turned into the waves away from the shore. The third man at the tiller alone seemed in his element, a hard-looking unshaven man with dark wind-tanned skin.

"Where are you taking me? Who are you and what right . . . ?" She started to question again.

"Shut up."

"I demand to know."

"You demand nothing. You do as you're told. They want to talk to you. You're a risk. You *were* a risk. That's enough for you," one of the men said.

"Who wants to talk to me?"

"Stop the chat." The man who appeared to be in charge, the one she thought she recognised from the attack in London, shouted at her. There was a long silence.

Fiona looked desperately back towards the fast receding shore. Already it was too far to think of swimming. They would pick her up straight away, and besides her sheepskin coat. . . .

It began to rain, and, with the spray breaking over the bow

as the motor boat forced its way through the waves, she was soon soaking and cold.

"Have you an oilskin?" she asked nervously.

One of the men threw her a tarpaulin. She pulled it round her tightly, noticing as she did so the gun which he still clenched in his hand.

They headed south-east. Ahead could be seen the faint outline of the mainland. The cloud hung lower and more threatening in that direction and the wind, picking up the rain with it, was building up white crests on the waves. The boat was making fairly poor going and was pitching and rolling heavily in the swell. Despite the tension in the situation, Fiona found herself yawning uncontrollably as a well-known warning of approaching seasickness. She noted with some comfort that at least one of her three abductors was already looking even greener and unhappier than she herself felt.

Attempting to take a grip on herself, she looked back towards the unheaving shore and then glanced at her watch. At a rough estimate it would take them at least an hour to cross to the nearest point, if that was where they were heading. They would hardly aim for one of the harbours and it was more likely to be at some deserted stretch of beach.

Where was she ultimately going, and why? Who were the "they" who wanted to talk to her and why was she a risk? It was about the Norsemen. Did they think she would have betrayed everything? If Calder had been at home, they would have been right. But now, she had been on the point of going back to them, dedicatedly and unquestioning. It was ironic and still incredible, yet here she was being kidnapped in the middle of Scotland in broad daylight. She shuddered and pulled the tarpaulin tighter round her shoulders. Callum would never have arranged such a thing. He would have been angry perhaps, but this was something bigger, something she still didn't understand. She thought of Axel and his mysterious source of funds.

After about ten minutes she gradually began to focus on a boat approaching to starboard, grey against the horizon, pushing up a powerful bow wave. The others hadn't noticed it yet, and it looked as if it might pass fairly close. If she were to . . .

The man at the tiller had seen it too now, and pointed it out to the others. The leader shrugged indifferently, and tapped his gun significantly. The message was clear. Any false move and he was ready.

Two or three more minutes passed. The other boat, a small naval patrol boat, was now clearly visible less than a quarter of a mile away and bearing straight at them. The leader called to the helmsman to pull out the throttle, but it rapidly became obvious that the patrol boat was altering course to follow suit. Fiona's heart was beating excitedly.

The leader spoke rapidly to Fiona: "If we're stopped, and they're probably on the look out for smugglers or something, not a word from you, d'you hear, or there'll be trouble. You don't get any ideas about trying for help. This thing's too big for me to be worried about using this, I can assure you."

"Ahoy! Reduce speed and come alongside." A loud-hailer from the naval vessel interrupted the man's warning.

"Bear over," the leader said reluctantly to the helmsman. "We'll bluff it out."

The two boats slowed down and, with some difficulty in the heavy swell, came within a few yards of each other. Fiona could see a naval officer standing by the bridge of the patrol boat. A civilian in yellow oilskins was beside him.

"What do you want? Careful or you'll swamp us!"

"Come along side. We're taking you in tow." The officer gave his order through cupped hands.

"What the hell's this about? We're fishing," the leader shouted back, casting a warning glance in Fiona's direction.

"You're under arrest. We have a warrant."

The leader reacted quickly and shouted to the helmsman: "They're on to us. Full throttle and make for the mainland. They won't risk ramming us and we'll run them out of depth at the river's mouth. They won't be able to go as far into the shallow water as we can."

As the little motor boat's engine shuddered into full gear, Fiona made a blind attempt to get over the side, but with a curse, one of the men pulled her roughly back into her seat. She sat there helplessly watching.

The motor-boat beat heavily through the waves, the naval patrol keeping easily alongside, with the officer continuing to shout commands at them to stop. Once it pulled a little ahead of them, and the wake of the larger boat caused the little one to toss violently. Fiona gripped the locker seat to steady herself. As she did so she felt the fuel pipe. Made of polythene, it ran from the tank in the stern to the engine amidships, tucked just under the locker on which she was sitting. Her captors, with only one eye on her, were anxiously watching the manoeuvres of the patrol boat. She gave a discreet pull at the pipe but it refused to give. She tried harder, it gave a little at a connection and she watched with satisfaction as petrol began pouring out over the deck. The men still hadn't noticed when the engine spluttered and died.

"—the hell? That bitch has got at the fuel pipe," the helmsman barked angrily. The boat had juddered to a stop, and with no headway on, was slewing about dramatically in the waves. The patrol boat ran up close beside them.

The leader of Fiona's abductors stood up and shouted at the naval officer. "Throw a line then, damn you. But you'll tow us where we want to go, and quickly, otherwise the girl gets it." He waved his gun so that there would be no doubt.

The naval officer could be seen turning to the civilian for guidance. But none was needed. Fiona took advantage of the suspense and threw herself over the side.

The icy cold hit her and she thought she heard a shot, but then her heavy clothes began pulling her down.

Victoria, Tuesday Morning

Walt Tesco was a fraction surprised when the receptionist at his scruffy hotel brought him a letter as he sat at the breakfast table.

He stared thoughtfully at the envelope for some minutes without opening it. A plain brown envelope, the address neatly typed and with a London postmark. Tesco was a poor correspondent at the best of times, but to receive this letter was all the more surprising since he had been working on the assumption that few people knew or cared where he was staying. It had required a certain amount of effort on someone's part to find out.

He forked the last of the greasy bacon and eggs untidily into his mouth, wiped his hands on a paper serviette and decided with a shudder to leave the rest of the so-called coffee. He picked the envelope up from the soiled tablecloth, dusted a few toast crumbs off it, and opened it.

Tesco's first reaction was that it would prove to be another piece of information planted by the Establishment for him to leak about the Norsemen, but this was quickly dispelled. The message, typed on a plain sheet of white paper, gave no direct indication of who had sent it. It was the blunt promise of interesting revelations and "proof" that would be sent to him about the real background to the Norsemen. It would come in time for inclusion in the following Sunday's press, and would demonstrate which was really the more honourable, the Norsemen or their opponents.

Tesco was intrigued. He didn't doubt the genuineness of the message since it showed too much skill for it to have been the work of a crank. Almost certainly it had come from the Norsemen side, but why to him? He thought for a moment of the girl. But it was inconceivable that she had done this. Then the man Axel? He might have overheard the conversation with the girl. Now he was dead, but he could well have passed on what he had heard to someone else.

Tesco didn't mind being the centre of attraction. If it was useful to him, he would be useful in turn. He got up from the breakfast table a little more quickly than he usually did. With what he had already garnered there were the makings of a big story. But that elegant buffoon Rossetti, who had lunched him the other day had threatened him, and if he was going to get further involved then he needed a protector as well as a story. He would have to choose his newspaper, or rather his newspaper proprietor, carefully. And first he had a few more researches to do.

ELEVEN

H.M. Prison, Wednesday Morning

The green-painted corridors echoed as they walked. One warder, keys jangling from a chain at his waist, walked ahead of them to open up the dividing gates, another came a respectful few paces behind. The assistant prison governor explained that the traditional hollow sound was something to do with the metal sheeting on the cell doors. The place was as cold and grim as any nineteenth-century institution and the assistant governor, in his rimless half-moon spectacles, matched its qualities well. He described how there were plans to build a new modern prison, more comfortable and less soul-destroying for the inmates, but he failed to say whether he himself would change to match the bright new style. MacCaig inwardly doubted it.

The procession mounted an iron staircase, which, with its bars hooped over the top to prevent suicides, appeared like an elongated birdcage. It halted briefly, while the assistant governor reprimanded a warder about a cigarette butt he had noticed lying abandoned in a corner. As they went on their way, MacCaig heard behind him the warder in his turn bawling abuse at a prison trusty for not being diligent enough in his cleaning.

They came to an iron grille which led to the women's wing. Two female warders took over as escorts to MacCaig and the assistant governor. Still the passages echoed as they walked, but the paintwork now was a dirty, though doubtless more feminine, cream. To the sound of their footsteps was now added the constant clatter of metal buckets on stone flagstones as inmates went through the daily process of scrubbing out already spotless rooms. Then there was the higher clash and jangle of tin plates on battered metal food trays and the heavy despairing clang of cell doors slamming shut and bolts being shot home. An indescribable smell of carbolic, unwashed bodies and the most pervading of all odours, boiled cabbage, hung in the air. Even in the central block, with its rows of barred catwalks stretching tier upon tier to the glass skylights high above, the smell persisted. It was cold enough, yet no really fresh air seemed to circulate.

Cell three-five-two. The wardress looked through the observation slot and then threw open the door. The cell, whitepainted brick, a chair, basin, trestle bed and high up, a little barred window set in the wall. Fiona was lying on the bed reading. She looked up woodenly, saw MacCaig and her eyes lit up a little.

"I understand you've to be left alone with her. A wardress will be right outside, so shout if you have any trouble." The assistant governor withdrew and the cell door clanged shut behind him.

"You heard, behave, or I scream." MacCaig feebly tried to joke.

"I don't think that's very funny. What's going on? Why am I here? Why are you here, Calder? I thought you were abroad. What right . . .?"

"Wait a minute. Wait, one thing at a time. May I sit down? I never reached the airport to go to Oslo, and I don't think I've stopped since."

She looked angrily at him, but he saw it was an anger close to tears. He perched on the wooden chair.

"But why am I here? What have I done? You must tell me. It's now three days since they picked me out of the water, and I haven't been allowed to contact anyone."

"I'm very sorry, Fiona. But you must understand that it is for your own protection."

"But of course I'm grateful for being rescued—from what I still don't know. But whatever it was, it couldn't have been worse than this . . . this foul place." She looked around desperately, her eyes watering. "Your people could have protected me in some other way."

"The other side are very determined."

"You seem to be a step ahead."

"Some of the time. But there's another reason for your enforced stay, about which, incidentally, I couldn't do anything even if I tried. We've put it about among your . . . friends that you've been arrested, that you've been very unco-operative with us and that should give you a clean bill of health when you're let out."

"You've no right . . ." She stood up angrily, her eyes blazing with frustrated rage.

"Sorry, let me finish," he said firmly. "*When* you're let out, I said. It may sound like a threat, but I have to tell you that you're to remain here unless . . ."

"Unless what?" She almost shouted the words.

"I hope you'll agree to help. I have some papers here which give the background. You'll see that while Callum and some of the others on Norsemen are on the level, are genuine in their beliefs," he corrected himself, "others, particularly Axel, are, were, I should say, not what they seem."

There was a pause, then: "Please don't start with that all over again. I couldn't stand it." Her momentary anger had subsided and once again she seemed about to cry. "And the way you just spoke about Axel—what's happened to him?"

"He, he had a car crash. He was killed instantly." MacCaig broke the news bluntly and without emotion.

She was silent for a moment then she said: "He was a hard, determined man but that's a dreadful thing."

"There would be no 'buts' if you'd seen the two men he got—an innocent bystander shot in the stomach and a policeman with a fractured skull who's not expected to live." He told her about the chase at the airport.

"But why did he run when he saw you?" She stared at him in bewilderment, her words now coming in a faint whisper.

"Because he had something big to hide and in some way knew I was on to him. I think he must have known even before I did, that I was going to be involved in this operation and he would certainly have had this confirmed by the evidence about me in some files that were stolen." He told her about the visitors to his uncle's farm and about the subsequent attack on Rossetti.

Fiona was profoundly shocked and looked it. She had less difficulty in believing MacCaig now; the grim surroundings helped to concentrate her mind.

"These papers: read them. You'll see where the instructions really came from—that alone will make you think. I hope when you're in the picture, you'll actually be willing to help us put a stop at least to the evil element, the murderers and would-be murderers in the whole operation." He looked at her hard.

"But I believe in it." She was sitting on the edge of her bed now, face buried in her hands. He stood up slowly.

"In its ideals, yes. So do I. So I think does the . . . so do others. But if you won't help, then, put bluntly, its been decided that you'll have to stay put until things are cleared up. That may take some time."

"That's a very honest threat." She looked up at him.

"I hope when you've read all this, you'll not feel threatened at all."

"So the paper that man Tesco gave me about the source of the money was correct?"

"Yes."

MacCaig waited a moment then suddenly turned and went over and banged on the cell door. The wardress opened it immediately.

"Calder. You're not leaving me here in this place . . . like this. Please . . . when are you coming back?" She had woken up to the fact that the interview was over and her eyes were wide and anxious. Then she was crying. He wanted desperately to take her in his arms, to comfort her, to tell her it would be all right, but the wardress, a large harsh-looking woman, stood impassively in the doorway.

"Tomorrow. Just twenty-four hours, Fiona." He tried to smile.

"Doesn't, don't I mean anything to you?"

"Yes," he said briefly, and then turned and left the cell. The door swung closed behind him, with a clang she had come to hate.

Westminster, Wednesday Afternoon

It was Question Time in the House and from the Opposition benches the Member for Tachwood, a bitter little man, stood up to speak. Question Time is an important, some say *the* most important part of the democratic system of Government—the answerability of Ministers to the rank and file. Too often, however, it deteriorates into a jousting-match between the participants and much more rhetoric and invective flow than facts and enlightenment. It calls for quick wit, strong nerves, and a modicum of good humour from the major participants. Question Time can make or break a Minister.

The Minister of State therefore glanced a fraction nervously at his brief which lay in front of him, neatly typed on its blue crested paper. Admittedly he knew what the first question was going to be:

"To ask the Secretary of State whether he has noted press reports about the existence of an an internationally-based organisation called the 'Norsemen', and if he will make a statement?"

It was one of those innocent-looking questions to which the Supplementaries, the follow-up questions which the M.P.s were allowed to ask, were much the most dangerous part. It had been stimulated by the little news item in the *Standard* which in turn was the result of Tesco's official briefing. While that operation had paid off, it now looked as if the publicity might backfire to the considerable embarrassment of the Government. The Minister had a short answer to the main question laid out in front of him, meticulously drafted and re-drafted by his Civil Servant underlings, but as to the Supplementaries, he and his Civil Servants could only guess.

The Minister braced himself and slowly rose to reply. The House was crowded and as he stood up, there was a sudden expectant hush among his colleagues. In a way peculiar to the House, they sensed something untoward was going to happen. The public in the Strangers' Gallery caught the feeling and craned their necks to get a better view. Even the Speaker, till then almost hidden under his wig, eased forward in his throne to listen attentively.

"The Secretary of State is unavoidably detained and I have been asked to reply," the Minister began. A mutter of rather cruel amusement rippled among his more aware colleagues. Old Arthur, the Secretary of State, still nominally in the chair, was for the high-jump today. They all knew it. The Opposition benches allowed themselves some subdued laughs.

"We have noted the reports in the press which the Member for Tachwood has mentioned, and the matter is being kept under constant review. It would not be in the public interest to say more at this stage."

The Minister sat down again quickly, knowing full well that he wouldn't get away with that bit of stone-walling. Four or five Members were on their feet each trying to catch the Speaker's eye. But the Member for Tachwood was allowed a further question.

"Is the Minister refusing to give Members of this democratically-elected House information on a subject which is a matter of considerable concern to a large number of people? Allegations reputedly stemming from Governmental sources that a respectable international political movement has been in some way infiltrated by forces opposed to the *status quo* in this country should be substantiated or denied."

There were noisy cries of "Hear, Hear from the Opposition benches, but the questioner wasn't finished. "I would go as far as to ask," he went on, "for a definitive Government assurance that other rumours circulating, which suggest that the Government has set out to destroy a perfectly legitimate political movement through calling into question its peaceful nature and the source of its funds, are without foundation. It would be a sad day if the Government of this country were to engage in underhand discrediting operations of a clandestine nature just because it doesn't like the political complexion of its opponents." Further noisy shouts of support for the questioner came from the Opposition benches. On the Government side there was a surprising, slightly embarrassed silence. The

Speaker called for order and obliquely reprimanded the Member for Tachwood:

"Would Members bear in mind that this is Question Time and that it is not the occasion for speeches or polemics." The Speaker's voice was thin and reedy, but it had authority behind it, and the Member for Tachwood sat down again, rebuked.

The Minister rose to reply. "I have nothing to add at this stage to what I have said already, except perhaps to say that we have reason to believe that certain forces inimical to democracy . . ."

He was interrupted by a burst of shouting and counter-heckling from both sides of the Chamber. For some moments pandemonium reigned. It was an issue that always provoked considerable feeling on both sides of the House, the suggestion that external forces were in some way involved against the State. The older members remembered the stories in the 'twenties about the Zinovieff letter, and in the 'sixties about the "small band of politically motivated men" who had stood accused of being inspired from abroad in their industrial strike activities. Such remarks had in the past led to the defeat of Governments.

The Speaker hammered for order and eventually the hubbub subsided. He rebuked the House severely for its disorderly behaviour. The Minister meanwhile had sat down again. With luck, he thought to himself, that was the storm over for today unless someone forced an emergency debate, and that was unlikely at the present stage, given the lack of public facts.

Unfortunately, the Speaker rather surprisingly allowed a further supplementary. The Leader of the Opposition, a gaunt, grim man who possessed the best nose in the House when it came to making political capital out of a scandal, was on his feet.

"Can the Minister deny totally and utterly," he demanded, "that he is in charge of an operation which has been set up by this Government with the express purpose of destroying the Norsemen? Can he also honestly deny that despite his, or perhaps because of his well known personal sympathies for the forces of nationalism north of the Border, he has been forced against his will into taking on a repellent overlordship, the robes of a Grand Political Inquisitor for reasons . . ."

Again the words were interrupted as the storm of heckling and cries of support broke out on both sides of the House. Back-benchers and front-benchers alike were on their feet waving their order papers. The Prime Minister had now appeared and was on his feet too, angrily trying to answer what had turned into an attack on him. After several more minutes of uproar, when the threat of closure had been made, the Speaker eventually managed to call the House to order and disallowed further questions on the same subject. The Leader of the Opposition quietly warned the Government that they would ask for an early debate on the Norsemen, and then, as suddenly as it had all flared up, the House and its Honourable Members subsided into amicable boredom once again, as they listened to the Minister of Agriculture talking about measures for curtailing a new outbreak of foot-and-mouth disease in the West Country.

The Minister sank thankfully back on the Front Bench not altogether unhappy at the way things had turned out. Everything was in the open now. The discredit, if any was to come, might with care be placed on more important shoulders than his own. He had been branded as the honest broker forced into doing a job he disliked. And that was true enough. It wouldn't endear him to his political master, his being in one way the cause of the rumpus, but that didn't worry him either. He couldn't care less if the P.M. got clobbered. All that had to be done was to avoid getting in the way when the club was swung.

TWELVE

Oslo, Friday Afternoon

The taxi climbed slowly up the steep side of the hill. In and out among the pines, the road, laboriously scraped clear of the remains of the winter snow, gave an occasional glimpse of Oslofjord stretched out below. The view had lost some of the majesty given it in the depth of winter, and had yet to gain the freshness of spring. On the hillside above the road were rich modern houses of white wood and granite, each perched with its own superb view amid extensive grounds, high above the mundane life of the city below.

Two men on skis passed them, riding easily across the hard-packed snow by the roadside beside where the great gutters ran that would carry away the rushing flood of melted snow at the first real thaw. The skiers moved with a minimum of obvious effort down the track that led through the woods to a ski-jump on the far side of the hill.

Fiona Ross and Calder MacCaig sat silently in the back of the taxi, each preparing for the act to come. There was little danger. Axel was dead and his three thugs who had attempted to abduct Fiona, were safely locked up in Pentonville. The people they were about to meet might not trust Fiona all the way, since Axel could well have reported his doubts about her, but they would have little immediate option but to accept her at her face value. Her arrest and the reports of how unco-operative she had been in prison had helped give her a new credibility among the rest of the committee, and Callum, confronted by the evidence, had reluctantly been persuaded to co-operate by writing a letter to international headquarters reporting Axel's "accident" and passing on his supposed wish that the treasurer's role go to her. MacCaig was hoping he too was superficially clean, despite what they must have known from the stolen files and from other sources which, he personally still assumed, they must have had access to. His employers had tended to discount the earlier evidence of the two men who had come looking for him before the files had disappeared. They had made some superficial and unsuccessful enquiries, and afterwards MacCaig had been as good as told that they now believed that his uncle must have misheard the reference to the Norsemen. He was far from convinced but he had more pressing matters to attend to. And even if they did know more, it would be difficult for anyone in Oslo to link him directly with a name in a file report, now Axel was gone. They certainly wouldn't expect him to turn up on their doorstep, billed as Fiona's strong man, there to give her support in case it wasn't all woman's work.

They had spent the night in separate rooms in a hotel in Oslo, and, on instructions, hadn't been in touch with the Norwegian security people. That was to come once they had established themselves. They had hardly talked together except over details of the operation and any gentler feelings between them had been put in second place, both of them for the moment seeking to forget the emotion of their final exchange in the prison. She, more determined than broken by the shattering of her ideals, was now fully committed to the role she had to play, believing that she owed it to her past beliefs and in no way relating it to her feelings for MacCaig. He was thinking of Tinker and the old scars on his body tightened his bitterness. He wished he had brought a gun, but he had decided to play safe, and perhaps it was as well.

The house stood well back from the road up a long drive lined by pines and silver birches. A palatial two-storey building, clean and white, conspicuously demonstrating the wealth of whoever owned it. A flag fluttered limply at the top of a tall flag-pole, indicating that the owner was in residence.

A severe-looking housekeeper showed them into the dark hall where they were greeted by a little weasel of a man who introduced himself as Herr Schoeyen, the owner. He appeared nervous and ill-at-ease, and was obviously at a loss as to how to respond to the immediate explanation of their presence. Then an inside door opened quietly and a man stood framed in the doorway against the light from the room behind him. He came towards them, smiling and welcoming, and introduced himself, "—name of Issouna, Stefan Issouna." They shook hands, formally. "Call me Stefan." He had been listening, he said. His English was perfect. "So sad, so dreadfully sad about Axel—such a promising young man and a great loss to us all." He looked as if he meant it.

They were shown into a large cold study. The nervous Herr Schoeyen had disappeared. The two visitors seated themselves round a big oak desk opposite their host whom they could now see more clearly in the bright electric light. Stefan Issouna seemed to occupy the entire space on the other side. A vast man with an almost bald head, large fleshy hands clasped together in front of him as if in prayer. He questioned them slowly and courteously. As he spoke he had a nervous habit of wiping his forehead from time to time with a white silk handkerchief. Then, seeming to appreciate what he was doing, would put it rapidly away, and reclasp his hands in front of him once again.

A maid brought coffee on a silver tray but the cross-examination continued gently and without a pause. Outside it was rapidly growing dark. At last, appearing satisfied with their credentials, particularly after hearing about Fiona's prison stay, Issouna stood up and showed them through into another room—more like a board room with a table down the middle, round which seven other people were sitting talking. The table was covered in paper, coffee cups and littered ashtrays. A meeting was in progress. They looked up as the three came into the room. Issouna explained the visitors with a few words. There were no questions and none were invited. It was obvious who was in control.

The meeting continued with the man they all called just Stefan, speaking slowly and in almost accentless English: "The attraction of a united Europe acts as a magnet does on iron filings. It draws most strongly those particles nearest to the centre of it. The remoter parts are relatively untouched. Now another magnet is pulling from the north-east and it is only natural that what were always considered 'the outer fringes' of Britain and of Europe should like to become 'inner' in their own magnetic field."

None of the other people round the table moved or spoke. All sat forward, listening intently. The man went on: "The trouble with political left and right alike, however, is that while they consider new nationalisms and new interdependencies a good thing for the third world, when it comes closer to home, their cry is about the danger of Balkanisation. Then it becomes something unthinkable and perverse."

The speaker's voice had sunk to a gentle and almost relaxing whisper. MacCaig glanced across at Fiona. She was sitting on the edge of her chair, eyes fixed intently on the big man as if hypnotised. Suddenly he raised his voice sharply and his tone changed. The atmosphere in the room was electric.

"This was the idealists' background. But idealists have never created, and now is the time for action—militant action. The authorities in the countries concerned are using every method, violent and otherwise, to suppress us. It is time to take off the gloves and enter phase two of operation Norslag. We have colleagues in high places and they will help us disrupt, dislocate, and finally remove the complacent outdated structures of governments in these countries."

A telephone bell rang somewhere in the recesses of the house. The speaker continued without a break: "We have already agreed a programme of physical sabotage, the creation of doubt, the playing on popular emotions and fears over racial and other tensions, these will be concentrated upon. This is the background. Now in more detail, here are some of the schemes . . ."

The speaker stopped as the nervous Herr Schoeyen came into the room.

"I have told you before. We are not to be interrupted," Issouna said angrily.

"But . . . but there's a long distance call . . . for you personally. They want you . . . it's most urgent."

The man reluctantly left the room. None of the other people remaining round the table spoke or introduced themselves to

Fiona or MacCaig. They might as well not have been there. The silence was almost frightening.

After a few minutes the man returned. He stood for a moment in the doorway and looked round at the assembled company. Then he smiled unexpectedly. He took out his handkerchief.

"I must apologise, but I have something most urgent to attend to. As we have been working very hard, may I suggest a break for dinner?"

Everyone stood up. Still no one else spoke. The man came smilingly up to MacCaig and Fiona Ross.

"Most of our colleagues are sleeping here. You, I understand, are in a hotel, but perhaps dinner? Good. Then let me show you the way."

He led the two through the hall and into a small cloakroom.

"If you'd like to refresh yourselves—there are towels here—then come through and have some sherry." He spoke for all the world like a host at a country house party. He bowed slightly and went out, closing the door quietly behind him.

"So far, so good," Fiona whispered as soon as he left. "Fascinating talk, if a bit more violent than I've heard before."

"I'm not at all sure. It's not the sort of thing I expected at all. It's too neat, too formal. It's almost as if they're putting on a show for our benefit," MacCaig whispered back. "Just a moment. I'll make sure no one's listening outside and then I'll tell you what I think."

He went to the door and tried to turn the handle. It was locked.

Pall Mall and Whitehall, Friday Evening

A tailcoated waiter balancing a large tray of drinks in one hand, collided heavily with a fat woman in a wide-brimmed hat. The resultant scene for a moment took much of the pomp and grace out of the Lancaster House Reception. A few people laughed but most of the guests pretended not to have noticed. The

Ambassador from some South American dictatorship, in immaculate evening dress, swept past unseeing, with his beautiful, diamond-bedecked wife in tow. Distantly but formally he greeted an African colleague in a way that signified that he had no desire to be drawn into conversation. The African diplomat, in turn, was more concerned with trying to charm a well-known, visiting American negress, a blues singer and was getting nowhere. Realising his limitations, he gathered his colourful robes around him in mock despair and, remarking laughingly to the world at large that the culture barrier was often more noticeable than the race one, went off in more successful pursuit of a sympathetic and frustrated Anglo-Saxon lady journalist. Eighteenth- and nineteenth-century dignitaries gazed down uncomprehendingly on the swirling scene from the vantage point of their portraits hung round the walls. A pair of uniformed ushers appeared discreetly with brushes and shovels to clear up the debris from the waiter's earlier catastrophe with the tray of drinks.

Rossetti had wedged-in some unwilling victim and was talking true to form in a corner behind one of the great gilt pillars in the Long Gallery.

"I don't like it, not at all, I don't. Very rude and unpleasant man MacCaig—and actually sleeping with this girl—who's on the other side so to speak, or was. Now they've gone off to Oslo together as if they were on a honeymoon—and with official blessing at that."

Rossetti's victim looked around hopefully for someone who would release him. The only people near enough at hand were the African diplomat and the woman journalist—and they were totally preoccupied with each other.

"Quite so." he said vaguely. He was more interested in what the African could possibly see in that cow-like harridan.

"The evidence is crystal clear. They, the nasty element in the Norsemen Organisation that is, were as windy as hell about her passing on what she knew, especially about where the money went and who the big backers are. It was a case of shutting her up at all costs, but they underestimated her. She got away from them but then they brought in two expert thugs who traced her pretty smartly to her island hideaway."

"Oh, I've just seen a friend. Would you excuse . . ." the victim interrupted weakly. But Rossetti was an expert Ancient Mariner.

"Luckily we had followed her ourselves, which allowed us to get the patrol boat organised pretty smartish and, after a little fuss, I understand we got them all. The girl was a bit damp but she dried out in prison. Now you've probably heard about the nasty accident at the Airport at the end of last week. The man killed was a local link man. High powered but not the real brains. Now he's dead and she's going over to Oslo to take his place—cool as a cucumber."

A waiter approached and Rossetti paused and turned to reach for a glass of champagne. The victim seeing his opportunity, pushed past and quickly away with a muttered "Excuse me, I must be going."

Rossetti shrugged and solaced himself with his glass. He leaned decoratively against a pillar musing to himself about the unnecessary rush most of his colleagues were permanently in. They so seldom had time to stop and talk. At one period in his life Rossetti felt that this might have been due to some failing in himself, that people might not like to talk to him. He had read the advertisements and tried changing his deodorant as a precaution. That had made no difference and he had therefore presumed simply that other people played life faster than he felt inclined to do. But once, closeted in a gentlemen's lavatory, he had overheard some of his colleagues discussing him in indelicately blunt terms. From then on he had allowed himself no illusions, but he was damned if he was going to change. He had felt momentarily embittered, then he learned to live with and capitalise on his habits and behaviour.

The reception was glittering, and Rossetti pretended to liking such occasions. Were he asked, he would say pretentiously that they added a touch of grace to the turgid drudgery of modern diplomacy. Receptions and similar festivities were enjoyment pure and simple, a slight compensation for hours spent shifting files from in-tray to out-tray. Any recipient of this wisdom would put it down as being "typical of Rossetti", and who was Rossetti himself to object to that? A touch more ridicule was of little consequence to him in present circumstances.

A discreet little man had appeared from the crowd to his right. Rossetti barely noticed him except to remark that he seemed rather out of place. The man was looking for someone. He stood incongruously on tiptoe, trying to see over the heads of the crowd. Then he spotted Rossetti, beamed and advanced on him. Rossetti shuddered. There must be some mistake. Then he recognised him as one of the messengers from the Office.

"Mr. Rossetti, Sir. Glad I've found you. Been looking everywhere. You're wanted urgently back at the Office."

"But it's nearly seven-thirty. It's Friday. I've finished for the week-end."

"Sorry, Sir. That's the instructions."

"Drat," said Rossetti testily.

There was a remote crisis on somewhere and Rossetti indicated his surprise at finding some of his colleagues still working. He hadn't realised anyone worked after six in the evening. The colleagues were not surprised since Rossetti always departed on the dot.

He walked noisily over to his desk, picked up the brown envelope with the big *Top Secret* label on it, and tore it open.

A flicker of distaste crossed Rossetti's face, and he put the piece of paper hurriedly down on the desk in front of him as if he had been burnt. Reaching into an inside pocket, he produced a silver cigar case and selected a long thin cigarillo with a slightly shaking hand. He seldom smoked before dinner. When he did, it was a sure sign that there was something seriously at fault.

A quarter of an hour later even his hard pressed colleagues had noticed that Rossetti hadn't uttered a word nor stirred from his desk. They passed unknowing looks and smiled enquiringly at each other at this unusually reticent behaviour.

Eventually Rossetti stood up, looked around him unseeingly, and then resolutely walked out of the room.

He was shown into the big oval room, and at once the Private Secretary discreetly withdrew. Fortunately the Minister had been working late as well.

"I'm sorry to bother you at this late hour, Minister, but I felt you should see this at once. It's the Norsemen again. We've been keeping track of the Oslo number that Axel telephoned and we picked up this transcript." Rossetti handed the Minister the piece of paper. As he did so, he noted with interest how tired and drawn the politician looked. Power wasn't a relaxing possession.

The Minister read it in silence. As he waited for him to finish, Rossetti allowed his eyes to wander across the top of the large leather-covered desk at which the Minister was sitting. The usual files and letters were there, all neatly arranged by subject, but in the middle of the blotter lay an open Post Office telegram. Like all good Civil Servants, Rossetti had learned at an early age how to read writing upside down. It was a handy attribute at meetings and conferences to be able to digest the brief of one's opponents sitting opposite. Almost without thinking, he deciphered the words.

"Call off tame journalist soonest. Essential immediate comply." The telegram was addressed to the Minister. The signature was obscured by a notepad lying on top of the telegram.

Then the Minister was speaking to him again in a low voice. Rossetti focused on him with a start.

"I beg your pardon, Minister, I didn't quite catch . . ."

"Do you know who is speaking from the London end?" the Minister repeated. He seemed to be talking with a great effort. The revelation that someone was betraying things had obviously shocked him deeply.

"'Fraid not, Minister. The machine went wrong and so we don't know who it is. But he seems to be well informed, you'll agree." An unusually hard look had appeared on Rossetti's face.

"And there's no way of finding out?"

"I understand that is definitely the case. But we could keep trying."

"No. No . . ." The Minister's voice was suddenly sharp. "No need for you to pursue the matter. Leave it with me. Is this the only copy of the monitored conversation?"

"Yes, Sir. In view of the delicacy, I have ensured that, and so far I have shown it to no one."

"Good. Very good. Then thank you. Thank you very much. Most grateful."

Rossetti appeared confused. The Minister was standing now, congratulating him, shaking his hand, saying that he had acted correctly, showing him to the door.

"But Minister. The message? What are we to do about that? It obviously refers to that man MacCaig and the girl, what's her name?"

"Miss Ross, Miss Fiona Ross," said the Minister precisely, opening the study door for him.

"Yes, Minister. They are obviously in danger, and there are security implications this end as well. I must report to . . ."

"Don't you worry about that. You have done your bit. You leave it entirely to me, and give me the transcript, if you please. One other thing; don't, I repeat, *don't* mention this to anyone else, will you. It would be very bad for morale. We must pursue this most cautiously. It could be exceedingly grave in political terms, you appreciate, especially after the fuss in the House."

Rossetti nodded wisely. He said he was glad he was in the Minister's confidence.

"It's most delicate, most," the Minister repeated almost to himself as he shut the door behind his bewildered visitor.

The Minister walked slowly across the oval room to his desk, sat down, and coldly and carefully began to re-read the paper that Rossetti had given him:

> "Stefan, is that you? Thank God I've managed to get hold of you at last. . . . What's that? . . . You were waiting for

me to call? . . . Oh, my God! Now look. Is it too late? . . . No, you know what I mean. Come off it, Stefan! I know. . . . Oh, thank God. Good. Stefan, please now, don't. Let's talk. I can't do anything directly, but I'll try my best to cool things off here. Meanwhile, there are two of our people, a man and a woman, coming in place of your man who was . . . who died at the Airport. Do you understand? Two people. You'll have to deal . . . That's enough, isn't it? . . . Good . . . Yes, Stefan. Yes. You won't ask me to do anything more, will you, Stefan? Not any more. Hello? . . . Stefan? . . ." The Oslo line had gone dead.

In his office, Rossetti was inelegantly biting his finger nails. Something seemed to be troubling him. Perhaps it was a remark recently said which jarred, which didn't ring true, or an ordinary G.P.O. telegram that suggested strange pressures. The Minister had been impressed by him, had said he had acted well. The Minister hadn't been worried about the danger the two in Oslo were in, nor about the leak. The Minister wanted to handle things on his own now, and perhaps he was right.

Rossetti found himself in a remarkably irritated frame of mind. He continued to bite his nails for some moments, then he reached for his telephone.

THIRTEEN

Oslo, Friday Evening

The door was a heavy affair of polished mahogany with solid brass fittings. He banged on it hard but there was no response. Bending low, he tried to look through the keyhole but could see nothing.

"It's jammed," he said in a loud voice for the benefit of anyone listening outside. But the look he gave Fiona belied his remark. He gestured to her to keep quiet and went up and whispered in her ear.

"They're on to us all right and they've locked us in. My bet is it was that 'phone call, though they could have suspected something before."

"What do we do?" she whispered back. She was pale, but showed no other sign of anxiety. He took her hand firmly to comfort her.

"Bluff it out. I'll bang again. If it's no go, we'll think of something. Don't start worrying yet."

"I won't. It's not something I boast about to my more revolutionary comrades," she forced a joke, "but I was born and bred with the Army. Kipling served with the cornflakes every morning."

"I knew there must have been a reason," he smiled back.

Five minutes of hammering and shouting produced no reaction. If it had been a mistake, the host would have noticed their absence before this. MacCaig turned and began to examine the little room. It served well as a prison. A windowless cloakroom, with a small W.C. leading off it. It too had no window, only a small ventilator set high in the wall.

"Conveniently chosen," he whispered. "I don't see any immediate way out."

"Then let's wait and see what happens," said Fiona simply. "They won't keep us here indefinitely, and they'll presume we're not here on our own. They'll let us out in due course."

"You're probably right." He didn't share her optimism, since they were unarmed and no one in Oslo knew where exactly they were. It would take a little time for London to realise that something was amiss, but he saw no point in worrying her further.

They sat down on the two plain heavy wooden chairs, which, along with a small paraffin stove and a wash-basin, were the room's only furniture. The house was centrally heated, though the temperature was kept low in deference to Issouna's wishes, and the paraffin stove was there in case of emergency.

MacCaig stood up suddenly and went over to the stove. He opened the top of the tank. It was full.

"Take these," he said, pointing to a pile of hand towels lying by the basin. "Soak them in water. Quickly. They may return any minute."

"What are you going to do?"

"Fire is the greatest enemy of people here. The houses are all wood. Ten minutes and a big house can be a heap of rubble. I've seen it happen in Iceland."

"You're not going to . . ."

"I'm going to burn our way out. The mahogany door won't catch for a bit, but the door frame is made of soft wood and it will, especially if it's soused in paraffin."

"But . . ."

"Get on with soaking these towels. We're going to wrap ourselves in them when they're wet; and soak your dress too." He picked up the little stove, went over to the door and began pouring the liquid carefully over the frame round the lock area.

She began methodically soaking the towels, piling them dripping on one of the chairs. It seemed all so unreal to her, despite her experiences of the past few days.

"Can't we wait?" She turned and started to argue.

"No! We must keep the initiative. Remember Axel, Tinker, though you didn't know him, and remember your own kidnapping. This isn't a game." He spoke harshly though keeping his voice low. "Are you ready?" He had produced a cigarette lighter.

"Yes," she said quietly.

"Then give me some of those towels."

She passed him a bundle and he put one over his shoulders, another he hung in front of him and he held a third for his head.

"O.K. Cover yourself too. It won't take long and then we'll be away." He knew there were a thousand dangers; of the door refusing to open before they were burned; of the people waiting outside with guns. He cursed his stupidity for not having risked bringing a weapon of his own. But to delay further would be to give the others time to get organised, time to find a way of disposing of Fiona and himself. Of that he was sure. He lit his lighter and applied it quickly to the door frame.

A wall of flame threw them back. Fiona felt the blast hit her. Together they crouched back in the doorway of the small W.C. wet towels shielding their faces.

"It will burn more subduedly once the paraffin has burnt itself out. See, the wood has caught already. Let's hope the people outside don't notice too soon."

MacCaig looked round rapidly, then leant forward and picked up a chair. The fire had begun to diminish somewhat after the first flare, but was still burning strongly. The wood round the lock was already heavily charred.

"I'm going to try now," he said. "It may be a bit early, though." He held the heavy chair in front of him.

At that moment there was a shout from outside and the door opened. Framed by the flames was the man Schoeyen, holding a gun. He was shouting hysterically. No one else seemed about and he had presumably been left to guard them alone.

MacCaig ran forward, brandishing the chair and the man brought up his gun to fire. Fiona's breath caught in her throat. It was too close range for there to be any doubt.

Then the remains of the paraffin in the little stove exploded in the heat and Schoeyen fell back as a chance chunk of metal hit him. MacCaig's jacket was on fire but he stumbled on through the doorway, shouting at Fiona to follow him. As he ran, he beat at his burning clothes with one of the wet towels.

They both got out into the hall. Schoeyen was lying motionless in the way. The fire had now caught the whole wall but was spreading slowly. Perhaps the wood had been chemically treated or the plaster work was acting as a break. But it had done its job.

MacCaig bent over the body and picked up the gun. "He's had it," he said indifferently. "Now let's get out of here." He slipped the gun in his pocket.

They went towards the main door and through into the garden. As they did so they heard voices and the sound of running feet. The explosion had been heard, where Schoeyen's shouts had passed unnoticed.

Outside it was dark but the moon had risen and, reflecting on the snow, provided just enough light for them to see.

"Over to these trees," shouted MacCaig. "They'll be after us in a moment and our prints will stand out on the snow. In among the trees we'll be more difficult to trace. Are you all right?"

"Singed hair, that's all. I always wanted my hair short." Fiona gasped. Her costume jacket was torn and black with the smoke, but apart from her eyes, which were still stinging from the heat, and the difficulty of adjusting to the darkness, she felt she had escaped remarkably lightly.

They reached the pine trees, and scrambled through them blindly. A branch whipped sharply across Fiona's face and she let out a brief exclamation of pain.

"We can take a rest. Quiet and listen." He leaned heavily against a tree taking the weight off his weak leg, and she could make out that he was clutching his shoulder where his jacket had been burning.

They peered back towards the house. Smoke was pouring from the main door and they could see figures running about wildly. Then three men appeared at the entrance. One was Stefan Issouna—they could tell him by his size. He had come outside on to the drive and stood framed against a window.

They could see the glow of flames in the house behind him. He started shouting orders and pointing to the two rows of their footprints running away from the house. The two other men began walking hesitantly across towards their hiding place among the trees. From the way they moved it was obvious that they were carrying guns.

"I don't want to use this revolver unless I have to. It'll give away our position," MacCaig whispered urgently, producing Schoeyen's weapon. "So let's get out of here fast."

Eyes now more accustomed to the dark, they moved fairly quickly through the pines and away from the house. Almost at once they hit the fence. It was about eight feet high, of thick mesh, topped with barbed wire and supported on concrete pillars, with the bottom firmly embedded in the soil. They moved their way down it, feeling their way slowly and trying its strength as they went. Behind them they could hear the sound of their pursuers gradually drawing nearer.

"I imagine this fence will go all the way round the compound, except for the gate, and they'll already be watching for us there. We can't climb it without being seen and I've nothing to cut through it with," MacCaig muttered.

At that moment Fiona slipped and fell. He couldn't see her for a moment, then realised she had stumbled into a ditch. Hidden by its covering of snow, it was a drainage trench about two feet deep, and it ran right under the wire.

"Are you O.K?"

"Just," came the muffled reply.

"Can you get out?" he asked anxiously.

"I think so, but wait a minute. The fence wire goes down a bit over the ditch but there's a small space underneath. We may be able to get through if we're lucky. It's bitterly cold, and I've lost a shoe." Her voice was strained.

He jumped down beside her, and one after the other they managed to scramble under and through into the wood beyond. When they climbed out, they were both desperately cold and numb despite their exertions. The temperature was just below freezing and their indoor clothes, still wet from their attempts to protect themselves from the fire, were rapidly icing over them.

Under cover of the trees, they paused for a moment and looked back. A gap in the trees just inside the compound threw up a silhouette of one of their pursuers who was standing uncertainly by the fence gazing about him. Behind him they saw with a sense of shock that the whole house was now firmly ablaze, the red glow and the smoke clearly visible between the trees.

They turned rapidly away from the house, hoping to find the road. He was almost carrying Fiona by now, since she was incapable of moving through the snow with only one shoe. He in turn was in pain from his shoulder injury and his bad leg was throbbing. After about a hundred yards, there was still no sign of the road and the trees were more thickly planted, making rapid progress impossible. The ground began sloping away steeply in front of them and he came to realise that they had completely lost their bearings in the flight. He desperately wanted to stop to rest but knew the dangers that would bring. The cold and snow would get them before their pursuers did.

"We must come across other houses fairly soon," he spoke reassuringly to Fiona, but he felt far from confident. They had passed several buildings on the way up in the taxi, but there was a lot of forest in the area, and once they had lost their direction, they could go for miles without hitting anything. Besides it was late by now and the lights in the houses would be out. They might pass very close to something in this densely wooded area without realising it.

Five minutes or so later they reached a clearing in the trees, in the middle of which was a ramshackle wooden hut, probably for the use of forestry workers. Its roof shone, ridiculously romantic, in the moonlight. Summoning a last reserve of effort, he dragged Fiona bodily over to it. She leaned thankfully against the wall while he tried the door. It had a metal catch on it but it wasn't locked and he pushed his way into the pitch black interior. It was empty.

By good fortune he still had his lighter and he struck it. It was indeed a woodman's hut. Benches, a table, a few tools and, most welcome, a couple of old duffle coats hanging by a nail on the wall.

He went outside again and dragged the now almost unconscious girl into the comparative shelter of the hut. He helped her struggle out of her wet clothes and into one of the thickly-lined duffle coats. There was a round cast-iron stove in the corner, and thankfully it was already laid with firewood. He managed to get it going without too much difficulty, and they both sat huddled round its growing warmth.

He realised it was dangerous staying so close to the house and also lighting a fire which might draw attention to their hideout. But he knew also that the immediate dangers of frost-bite and pneumonia were more telling. Besides, the people at the house were likely to be more than fully occupied with their own much larger fire.

After half an hour or so, he ventured outside in search of more wood, which he discovered stacked against the side of the hut, already cut into logs. As he came back in carrying a bundle, he thought he heard something moving in the forest behind him. He turned, reaching for his gun, but there were no more sounds and he relaxed again, went inside and shut the door. Fiona was already asleep, huddled on a bench by the fire, looking pale and worn inside the dirty coat.

He laid some more wood on the fire, sat down and in a few moments, he too was asleep, oblivious to the dangers of recapture in the soporific atmosphere of returning warmth.

Southwark, Friday Night

Tesco had followed the instructions diligently. It was the precise time and the precise place, but no one was there to meet him.

He had received the second letter that morning, a follow-up to the anonymous first. It too was unsigned, but told him that the information would be passed to him that evening. The place, a cluttered alley by the docks on the south side of the Thames, was, he thought, a bit unnecessary but he had merely been given the address and it was only when he arrived that he began to get second thoughts about the chosen rendezvous. It was the sort of location which conjured up memories of a Hitchcock film sometime seen and forgotten.

But Tesco was a journalist, and journalists he knew, usually stood well on the fringes of events. They passed on the processed news but they hardly ever got involved. He was all right. Besides, it had taken him a hell of a time and a pound to the reluctant taxi driver to find the place, and if he wanted the news he could hardly afford to be choosey. In any case, there was a friendly-looking dockland pub just across the way, and despite its darkness, the alley was relatively well lit. He'd be all right.

He stood under a street lamp and looked at his watch. It was exactly on the hour now. At that moment a car appeared at the far end of the street. This would be them, he thought, whoever "they" were. Why they couldn't have saved the dramatic setting and enclosed the information with their morning's letter he wasn't sure.

The car came up to him and stopped. It was a police squad car. The window wound down.

"You waiting for something?" the Officer in the passenger seat said officiously.

Tesco put on his middle-European accent. "I just make a story about London by night. I . . . a journalist."

The Officer got out of the car. "Any identification?"

Tesco produced his press card. The Officer glanced at it briefly. "Sorry. Can't be too sure. There've been a lot of warehouses broken into about here. And watch your step if you're carrying any money. A lot of the young lads about here have time on their hands; the skinheads—you heard of them? Well, there have been one or two people attacked, especially . . . er . . . visitors."

"I . . . O.K." Tesco said, smiling. "The pub over there, they have what you call 'drag show'. I do a piece for my paper."

"You're wrong there, mate. These drag pubs function closer into the City. Bloody dull if you ask me."

"That taxi man he say me . . ." Tesco lied and acted angry.

"You've been had. Most taxi men are on the level. You want a lift to the tube?"

"Now I here, I take a drink. Most kind," Tesco replied bitterly.

"Just as you like." The Officer shrugged and got into the squad car again. "But remember what I said." The car drew smoothly away.

In case they were looking, Tesco made a motion of going towards the welcoming lights of the pub. When the car disappeared, he retraced his steps back to the lamp post. His contact was late now, if it wasn't a fool's errand. But, of course, they would have stayed out of the road while the squad car was about. He'd give them another few minutes and then really go for a drink.

The tall windowless walls of the warehouses towered hostilely above him. The great gates, scruffy name signs illegible above them, were chained and barred like prisons. He could hardly imagine that in day time the alley could be bustling and alive. Now, there wasn't a single other person to be seen. Who the clientèle of the pub across the way could be in the evenings, he couldn't think, but he could hear the tinkling sound of an untuned piano and occasional voices and laughter. Behind these grotesque sightless warehouses must be houses or flats where people lived. They were well hidden.

He heard the distant sound of a barge hooting on the river, and then behind him he heard the creak of an iron gate. Despite his detachment, the sound made him shiver slightly. He wasn't a brave man, and in these surroundings, he was very much out of his element. He forced himself to turn to look in the direction of the sound and a cat bounded across the alley and in through a crack in the wall where a drain ran. He smiled to himself for his fear. What one did for one's living. But enough was enough. He looked at his watch again, then walked determinedly towards the pub.

He was still about twenty yards from it when the youths appeared from a side entrance. Five or six of them, he hardly glanced in their direction at first until something about the way they were staring at him made him speed up his pace towards the pub door.

He was a fraction too late. They moved across quickly in front of him, spread out in a line. They all looked much the same: closely cropped "skinheads", shirts despite the cold, and tight trousers suspended ridiculously at half mast by braces. They wore high lacing boots and all had their hands in their pockets. One had a little pork pie hat stuck carelessly on the back of his head. Probably not one of them was over twenty.

He scarcely hesitated but continued to make for the pub door. If these were the youths the policeman had mentioned, he was safe enough, only a yard or so from the warm lights of the pub. But they continued towards him, menacingly, hands still pocketed. One of them deliberately kicked a stone which was lying in the gutter. It nearly hit Tesco's leg, and he had to jump to avoid it. The boys laughed.

"Hey!" he said angrily. He might have said more, but at that moment, the one with the hat called out:

"Sorry Guv', no offence. You ain't by the name of Tescer, are you?"

"Yes," said Tesco automatically and immediately regretted it. His mind was working too slowly in the circumstances. These skinheads shouldn't know his name.

They came at him together. One of them, a grin on his spotty face, swung a boot without warning straight at Tesco's groin and found perfect contact. There was little need for the others, but they came in, feet swinging, nonetheless.

"Too sodding easy for a fiver", he heard one say, as the screaming pain ran through him, and then there was darkness.

FOURTEEN

Oslo, Saturday Morning

In winter, the Norwegian dawn comes late, and it was scarcely light when the men burst into the hut. Three or four of them, with Issouna in charge. MacCaig and the girl, stiff with cold, were scarcely awake when they were pulled roughly up from their benches and made to stand up against the wall. In the confusion, MacCaig felt his pistol slip from his pocket and it clattered down noisily on the bare wooden floor. One of the men bent down and picked it up while the others covered them with their guns. But there was little for the newcomers to worry about. As they forced themselves back to frozen reality, neither was in the mood to resist.

"Search them. See if they are carrying anything else." Issouna spoke unemotionally. One of his colleagues stepped forward and expertly frisked them. He laughed shortly as he saw that Fiona had more or less nothing on under the old duffle coat.

"They're clean, Stefan. Now what?"

"This is as good a place as any to find out what they're up to. The house is destroyed and it would be an inconvenience to have to transport them over to the house by the fjord now."

"But you said you knew who they were, that you had been told by . . ."

"Shut up," Issouna barked. The other man lapsed into anxious silence. There was no doubt who was in charge.

MacCaig was gradually regaining control of himself. Apart from being bitterly cold, and having an ache from the burn on his shoulder, he was feeling not too unfit. Inwardly, however, he was cursing himself for his ridiculous carelessness. He had got them both into this mess by not being more alive to the continuing danger. He cast a surreptitious glance at Fiona. She was standing against the wall, head down, clutching her coat around her. At first he thought she was about to pass out, then he noticed that her eyes were wide and alert. They both stood silently and waited.

"You!" Issouna jabbed at MacCaig with the shooting-stick he was carrying. "Explain yourself while there is still time. You burnt the house down, and the owner is dead. You have a lot to answer for on that account alone. I should hand you over to the police."

MacCaig looked straight at the man. He was almost tempted to smile at the mention of the police but said nothing.

"Very well then. I see we will have to apply pressure. You have come to spy on us, to destroy us, but fortunately we were warned, so we can be in first with the destroying." He almost hissed the last words out.

MacCaig looked again at Fiona. Her head still hung down. Momentarily he allowed himself to wonder about who could have informed on them.

"Let me make myself clear. But I will only do so once. I am not in the habit of wasting time, nor of compromising. I want to know what you are doing here, who knows you are here, and . . ."

"Quite a shopping list," MacCaig broke in evenly. His voice was dry and cracked. "But I rather gathered from your friend that you know it all already."

"Not the details, and insolence will get you very short shrift. Now start talking."

MacCaig slowly shook his head.

"Bring the girl over to the stove." Issouna addressed one of the other men. "The fire is pretty low, MacCaig. You've been careless here, too, but it will serve my purpose." He bent down and opened the fire grate. The embers were still glowing. He poked the ferrule of his shooting stick inside and waited a moment before withdrawing it again. Then he went up to Fiona and pulled open her duffle jacket.

"Now MacCaig. I am a professional. I shall begin very

gently. This isn't very hot, because I don't want to spoil my stick, and because I don't believe in the use of unnecessary violence. I'm sure you share that view." He jabbed it forward a fraction, and MacCaig heard Fiona's sharp intake of breath as the hot metal brushed against her.

"You know, so why the hell are you asking?" shouted MacCaig. "I'm here to catch a group of murderers and worse who have undermined a perfectly respectable movement. . . ." He checked himself and when he went on it was in more measured terms. "You are not interested in Norsemen except for your own interests. You have used . . ."

"I'm not here to listen to sermons. But you are right. Norsemen, if it had succeeded, would have been directly counter to our interests."

"Who are you? Which country are you working for?" MacCaig retorted.

"I work for one country today. But does it really matter? Yesterday I worked for another. I am a professional, a professional like you, MacCaig, but with perhaps less ties. As a mercenary I work for whoever pays the tune, you must know that MacCaig. Just a moment ago it was you who was asking me why I bothered putting questions to which I knew the answers."

"You wanted confirmation. You don't trust your source, is that it?"

"You are a clever man, MacCaig. Now go on." The man turned back to the stove, and again gently inserted the tip of his stick into the embers.

There was a knock on the door, and one of the other men came in hurriedly.

"There's a group of woodmen coming up the path towards the hut. They'll be here in a minute. What shall we do?"

"Keep them talking for a little. I'll come out and speak to them. Tell them anything—about the house fire for instance. But bring me in my briefcase first."

The man went out and reappeared in a moment with a black leather briefcase which he handed to Issouna. He disappeared again and they could hear the sound of talking outside.

"Not a word from you two," Issouna said. As he spoke he opened his bag and took out a little chromium-plated box. Out of it he took two phials and a hypodermic syringe. "In case you are worried, MacCaig, I used to be a doctor, once upon a time. A friend of yours, a man called Tinker found out about that and one or two other things about me. That's why he had to go. And I assure you that I still dislike unnecessary violence." He smiled emptily and then, carefully inserting the needle of the syringe into the rubber neck of one of the phials, he drew back the plunger. Fiona, head raised now, was watching as if hypnotised.

"Hold them. MacCaig first," the man ordered in a low voice. MacCaig was seized from behind by two of the men and started to struggle, but a gun was placed hard against his temple and he stopped, watching with horror as Issouna pulled back his sleeve and gently inserted the needle.

"Don't worry," said the man helpfully. "It's just a short sleep." Almost at once MacCaig began to feel relaxed. He was aware of himself smiling stupidly at the sight of the man's bedside manner. He watched him bending over Fiona, then going to the door. He heard him talking to the woodmen about the fire, about the two people in the hut suffering from shock and exposure. Then there was nothing.

Southwark, Saturday Morning

Somewhere, sometime some years before, Tesco couldn't quite remember when, there had been a similar sort of unpleasantness. He had been on a small boat with a press photographer. The other man had a camera with an extremely powerful telescopic lens. Despite that, they had gone too close to the big motor yacht anchored in the bay. But they had picked up the gossip about this shipboard romance and it would have been worth a lot of money. Tesco was there to write the story. The photographer had taken a long shot of the film star sunbathing in the nude, and then stupidly they had gone in for a close-up. But the man, the very famous man she was with, had seen them through his binoculars and was very angry. There had been several of the yacht's crew and a powerful hose. Their little boat had capsized. There had been a lot of people standing by the rails of the big motor yacht, laughing. For Tesco it had been a long swim back to the shore, and he had learnt his lesson.

This time the warning-off was less glamorous. He had come-to in the gutter where they had left him. He had tried to move and had immediately vomited. He couldn't even move away from it and passed out again. Two people had come out of the pub. How long had he been lying there? They looked down at him. "Disgusting," one of them said. "Some people can't hold their bleeding drink. Serve him bleeding right." They walked on and left him.

The publican had come out later to put up the shutters. He came across to the prostrate figure and peered curiously down at him. The publican knew his clientèle and also knew it was a long way to the next pub. He saw the torn jacket and guessed something of what had happened. He left Tesco where he lay and went to telephone. He'd do his duty and tell the police. But they could clear up the mess.

Tesco had become vaguely aware of two men talking about him through a field of pain.

"It's O.K. fellow. The ambulance will be here any minute."

Tesco opened his eyes and saw the policeman from the squad car, to whom he had spoken earlier. The publican was standing in the background. He was saying that Tesco had never been in his pub, and that no, he hadn't seen or heard anything. Nothing at all, nothing. Tesco tried to move, to speak, and was sick again. In the distance the siren from the ambulance echoed between the high black walls of the warehouses.

Later, lying washed and bandaged in his own bed on Saturday morning it wasn't quite so bad. No bones broken, just a mass of bruises and lacerations. Not even concussion, the doctor at the casualty station had assured him. Tesco had given a statement to the police. Most of it was true. It was certainly a fact that he had lost his wallet, and they didn't think to question him further. They had warned him, they said smugly.

Thinking about the events of the previous night, Tesco was merely inconvenienced by the loss of his wallet. His spectacles miraculously had remained unbroken. The publican had found them lying in the gutter and had sent them along with the ambulance. But Tesco was more than inconvenienced by the thought that the skinheads had known his name, that one of them had said that it was hardly worth the fiver. Someone had warned him off just like the time with the photographer and his telescopic lens.

But who? The Norsemen, presumably. And why? Was it because he had done that man Rossetti's work and tried to persuade that girl Fiona Ross? But how could they have known about that? Unless someone had been listening to him talking to her. More likely they had found the source of the original story in the German press, the one the British papers were now so worked up about. It would have been quite easy to trace it back to him.

They were on to him. They had taught him a lesson. Or had they? It made the story all the more interesting, and in his way, Tesco, though not a brave man, was not easily put off. But he was realistic, a realism reinforced by his present painful state and the memory of the previous night. If he was going to do anything further, then he couldn't go on acting on his own. He was more than ever convinced that he needed backing. He thought briefly of approaching the Establishment, of asking Rossetti and the Minister what it was all about. But that would be no use. There would be no final story for him if he went to them. They'd certainly muzzle him up because of the political fuss which was going on at the minute. After the storm in the House of Commons during Question Time, there would be no more stories, especially dramatic stories about a foreign journalist being beaten up, unless they had official blessing. No, he would have to find another ally.

Tesco eased himself up gently from his bed and picked up the telephone. He got through to the newspaper offices quickly enough. It was more difficult persuading the operator to put him through to the press Lord, Lord Allenford, but he persisted, and in the end he was successful.

FIFTEEN

Oslo, Saturday Afternoon

". . . Must say this is the best . . . rest I've had in years." Calder MacCaig moved himself slowly and luxuriously into a more comfortable position in the bed. He was vaguely aware that his words sounded muffled and blurred as if he were drunk. Not that he thought it mattered much. They blended rather well with the sound of waves breaking somewhere in the background and he felt warm and secure in the bed. With a considerable effort he turned his head and looked at Fiona who was lying in the next bed. He smiled stupidly at her.

"Don't you realise it's those injections. I feel as weak as a kitten." Fiona too found it an effort to speak, but her mind was oddly clear. Perhaps her dosage had been less potent.

"What does it matter, nice rest, nice, nice and quiet," he mumbled. For a moment the whole white-painted room seemed to revolve drunkenly, faster and faster like a roundabout. He shut his eyes tightly and his reluctant fingers attempted to grasp for stability against the soft mattress. At length he opened his eyes and all was still once more. The peace and cleanliness, something like a hospital room; beds of white painted steel; small softwood tables; bare, immaculately polished floors. A carafe of water and a glass stood on the commode beside each bed. A heavy ornamental jug sat on another table by the white-painted door. Chintzy curtains partially obscured the view of snow outside the window, as did the metal bars that were fitted securely into the wall. It was a perfectly adequate prison.

"Calder, for God's sake keep a grip. We're in prison here. Remember the fire, the house and the cold. *Remember*."

"Finest prison I've ever been . . . in." Calder felt it odd that she should be so ungrateful. He felt so relaxed, so much at peace. He could lie like this for ever, listening to the waves. But yes, he remembered the cold, like a dream. An unpleasant dream. Life was like a dream. And the man, Issouna, with the gentle hands holding a hypodermic. He had hardly felt a thing when the needle went in.

Fiona looked across at him. One good effect of the drug injection was that it had softened the hard embittered lines around his face and eyes. Lying on his back staring emptily at the white ceiling he looked relaxed and almost handsome once again. Fiona's eyes softened too. She tried to raise herself on her pillow but the strength had been taken away from her. So she lay, watching him instead.

"Calder, what are we to do? Calder, are you awake?" The words came slowly from her.

"Wait and see, Fiona. There must be a reason."

Fiona was aware that as they had been speaking, the door had opened and a figure in a white coat was blocking her view of MacCaig. She managed to move her head fractionally and looked at the newcomer.

"So you're both awake are you?" Stefan Issouna said. To their doped senses his voice sounded loud and rapid. Two pairs of eyes gazed vacantly back at him.

"I'm glad of that," he went on. "I wasn't very sure how long total unconsciousness would last, and I hoped you would come round before I left. The second stage, physical and mental, shall we call it relaxation, will also be with you for some time. I imagine it's still fairly effective. Let me see." He leant forward suddenly and jabbed his fingers at MacCaig's eyes. The eyelids didn't blink until some seconds later.

"Very satisfactory," said the man thoughtfully. "I hope you are comfortable. Not too hot, I imagine. I had the central heating turned very low. I prefer it that way myself."

"What are you going to do with us?" Fiona's voice came low and slowly.

"Ah, you can speak coherently already, Miss Ross. I make that about nine hours since the injection. Quite reasonable. But to answer your question; you are here as my guests for some time. I need your presence. It may be that I shall require you alive as a lever on your employers."

"Hostages for what?"

"You are curious, Miss Ross. Perhaps your friend Mr. MacCaig can guess." MacCaig lay still and said nothing. His eyes continued to stare vacantly in the direction of the speaker. "No? But then I think I gave him a rather larger dose than I did you, and he's not quite with us yet. I require you as hostages for the good behaviour of a man whom I need to keep under control."

"But how is this man, whoever he is, going to be influenced by our existence?"

"Because he feels or will feel himself directly responsible for your deaths, Miss Ross."

"What? Who is he?" she asked remotely. It all sounded so unreal.

"I think his official title is . . . no matter. You are too curious," the man answered quietly.

Fiona lay trying to make some sense out of what the man was saying. Her brain refused to produce any immediate answer and she started to speak again. But the man silenced her.

"No more questions. I have a plane to catch. I am going to London now and while I am away, the housekeeper here, who is also a trained nurse, will be in charge of you."

A middle-aged woman, pitch-black hair pulled back severely into a bun at the back of her head, swam into Fiona's line of vision.

"One injection every eight hours to be on the safe side, Madame, and five milligrams more for the man." Issouna passed on the instructions. "I should be back by Wednesday if all goes well. You have everything else you need, and the others are on call to help should the occasion arise."

Fiona heard the door shut and there was silence. She turned to look at MacCaig.

"I took it in," he whispered. The words came with surprising clarity. "Now I'm beginning to see a little more clearly. A man who might feel responsible for our deaths. That telephone call.

I think we may be able . . ." His voice tailed off into a whisper.

"I don't understand, but I'm so relieved you're not as bad as you seemed," Fiona said, "I was worried. Can you move yet?"

"Not very well I'm afraid, and that woman will be back at any moment to pump us full again."

Fiona watched helplessly as he struggled to sit up. He looked pale and weak. He had hardly reached a vertical position when the door opened and the housekeeper came in. She gave a shout and Issouna immediately reappeared as well. He came over to the bed and easily pushed MacCaig back against the pillow.

"So. More play acting, Mr. MacCaig? Well done, if I may say so. A true professional like myself. You'd better strengthen the dose and make it every seven hours, not eight, Madame. They obviously have more resilience than I thought." He had produced a hypodermic. The needle went in easily under the skin, and in a moment there was darkness once again.

Fleet Street and Vauxhall, Saturday Night

Tesco was feeling better. After all his efforts in persuasion, it was past the deadline for the Sunday first editions, but Lord Allenford hadn't come through with the go-ahead. The Editor had held the space for as long as he could. For some reason they had been deprived of a good story and it looked as if someone had been buying someone else off. It wasn't via Lord Allenford; that he had had direct from the man himself, and the promise of support had been genuine enough. Tesco was sure of that. Still the Establishment could be difficult when they tried.

Tesco eased himself gingerly down at an empty desk in the sub's room. He still felt exceedingly fragile after his beating up, but his basic constitution must have been sounder than he had believed. A bandage round his hand, and a plaster over the three stitches on his cheek was all that showed. He had got off lightly. He fished into his pocket for a battered packet of cigarettes, selected one and stuck it into his mouth, but didn't get around to lighting it. Instead he stood up thoughtfully, took his mackintosh from a hook behind the door and went out into the cold night.

A great slum of a block of flats, just south of Vauxhall Bridge. Most of the ground-floor windows had been boarded up against the ubiquitous attentions of vandals, but it was a hopeful sign that Authority might soon be coming to demolish the whole building. Overflowing garbage cans were stacked round the bleak courtyard and more stood by the brick huts in the middle that contained the outside lavatories for the flats. A cat screeched its love song in the background, cutting through the more human shouts of some domestic quarrel closer at hand. A teenage couple clung uncomfortably together in a dark corner by the common entrance, learning the hard way what life was about. Tesco pushed past them with an unnecessary and unwelcome apology, went blindly inside and then up an evil-smelling staircase with hardly any lights, that suggested something out of Dickens. He hammered on one of the two brown chipped doors on the top floor. A wizened old woman opened the door a chink. Tesco could see a burglar chain stretched across the gap.

"What yer want?"

"Is Callum . . .?"

"No." The door shut quickly with a bang, and Tesco was left blinking in the gloom. With the plaster and bandages he wasn't the most reassuring of sights. He wasn't prepared to try again so he turned, resigned to go. Then he noticed that the brown door opposite had opened a crack and a pair of wild looking eyes stared out at him. A second, almost identical looking old hag was watching him from behind her burglar chain.

"I was looking for Callum," he began hopefully.

"I heard. But you won't find him. They've put 'im away. I knew they would one day. That'll teach that old bag across the way." A malicious chuckle echoed through the crack.

"Away?"

"Wandsworth. Political activities, I hear. And about time too. Queer bloke. Always was, queer as that old tick of a neighbour of mine."

There was a noise in the staircase below and the second brown door slammed shut. Tesco shrugged to himself and began down the stairs. He heard footsteps coming up towards him as he went down. Then the noise stopped and whoever it was turned and went on down ahead of him.

He paid little attention to the sound, immersed as he was in thinking out the meaning of this new piece of intelligence. So the man Callum, whom he had been told was nominally in charge of the Norsemen, was in prison. Axel was dead, so that left a handful of Committee members who were probably unimportant, and the girl, Miss Fiona Ross.

He turned out of the block into the fresher air of the rubbish-filled courtyard and then into the street in search of a taxi.

He heard hesitant steps behind him. "Oh God," he thought immediately. "Not again. They're not going to get me again. They can't know yet what I said to Allenford."

Then a voice said: "Mr. Tesco?"

He turned round slowly, nervously clenching his fists.

"Oh, it's you, is it. What the hell d'you want?" Tesco, relieved that it wasn't another group of skinheads, hid his relief in an outburst of irritation. He glared balefully at the man who had come up silently behind him in the dark street. Rossetti's normally immaculate tie was askew, and the Etonian plastered-down hairstyle was distinctly ruffled.

"I've, I've been following you. I wanted to . . ." Rossetti began hesitantly.

"It's a pick-up then is it?" Tesco allowed himself a pun. He had been badly frightened and it was reassuring to see Rossetti appear confused. The pale light from a street lamp showed up the apparent anxiety on the other's face.

"No, I wanted to speak to you privately. You've been in a fight, have you?" Rossetti noted the bandages.

"Very observant. But you must have been on your way up to that man Callum's flat too. I heard you on the stairs." Tesco was further relieved at the other man's ignorance. His second thought had been that this was a prelude to the deportation he had been threatened with, that Rossetti might already have known about his *agent provocateur* role having been revealed to Allenford.

"No, that is, I knew he wasn't there, that you wouldn't find him. I was following you. You walked past me as I was on the way to see you at your Fleet Street office."

"Why didn't you stop me then?" Tesco was properly intrigued now. Rossetti cut a very different figure from the arrogant buffoon who had given him the lunch a week or so before.

"I wanted to find a more discreet place."

"I do believe it's because you're scared of something," Tesco said suddenly. "It took you some time to summon up courage. That was it, wasn't it? What's biting you?" The questions were framed in a slightly kinder tone.

"Can we go somewhere?" Rossetti looked round uneasily at the almost deserted street.

"Very well. There's a pub at the end of the street and it's still an hour till closing time."

They walked in silence towards the pub, each deep in his own thoughts. It was a grim brown-painted place with hard wooden chairs. The row of houses in which it stood was obviously scheduled for re-development, and, even though it was a Saturday night, it was almost empty. Most of the pub's traditional clientèle would have been slum-cleared away to one of the big modern slum estates further south.

Tesco bought two whiskies and a couple of halves of bitter without even consulting the other man. He had decided that this was a case to be followed up with a little bit of authority. They perched themselves at a secluded corner table and after a few minutes, when the interest shown by the barman and the other few guests in the peculiar pair of new arrivals had waned, Tesco leaned forward and said softly:

"What is it you're afraid of?"

"I'm not quite sure. It's entirely a personal thing, that's why

I thought you . . . It's the Norsemen business, of course. It's got frightfully vicious. I've suffered too." Rossetti stared almost enviously at the dramatic-looking plaster on Tesco's cheek.

"The man Axel was killed."

"He killed himself. But how did you know?" Rossetti looked up. "Well, I don't suppose it matters. That's past. It's the others that are the worry now." He shrugged.

"The girl, Miss Ross?"

"Yes, and the man she's with—MacCaig. Nasty bit of work, but still. They're in Oslo now and it looks as if they're in trouble."

"But your people can get them out of that. The massed authority of the State can surely do something."

"But authority doesn't know they're in trouble, at least not at official level."

"Then hadn't you better tell them?"

"I can't. I was told not to, and I'm unhappy about it."

"I can see that. It's because of the traitor in the works, isn't it?"

Rossetti sat up, shock written all over his face. "I didn't say that," he said sharply.

"You've just confirmed it."

"How did you know?"

"A journalist has his sources." Tesco said unhelpfully. He was going to fish, and the first rule of fishing was not to say what the catch was already.

"Then you think they have something on him?"

"Yes," Tesco lied blindly, wondering who was being talked about.

"What is it? It must be something pretty vile."

"What's your theory?"

"I haven't got one. It's all so unsure, and that's why I haven't told anyone else at the office. I might be making a fool of myself. It doesn't do one's career prospects much good to make unsubstantiated accusations."

"So you break the Official Secrets Act by telling me instead?"

Rossetti sat pale and silent for a while, looking down at his elegantly manicured fingernails.

"You will help?" he asked, looking up suddenly.

Tesco had seldom seen a man who appeared so close to a breakdown. He nodded kindly.

"It was when I was beaten up and the files were stolen, that I first suspected. Someone in his position doesn't usually ring up a junior official directly, you know."

Tesco didn't know. "Tell me all about it from the beginning, but first let me get another round."

"It's my turn," said Rossetti distantly.

SIXTEEN

Westminster, Monday Night

For the best part of the past hour the Minister had been trying to find out where Allenford was. His Civil Servants would have done it, as they had prepared his brief on the subject, but he had said he would try the personal approach first. They had told him of the enormous scandal that would follow, now that Tesco was threatening to reveal that he had been used as a stool pigeon. As if he didn't know. But Tesco was now under the protection of Lord Allenford, and as an individual didn't matter any more. Allenford was the key, and the Minister knew he would be a difficult one to turn. Still it had to be tried for more reasons than one, and urgently.

At last the Minister found out that the man was in the House of Lords, not fifty yards from the Minister's own room in the Commons. He cursed his stupidity for he had known well enough that the Lords were debating the Monopoly Commission Report on the press and he should have realised that Allenford was bound to be there.

He sent a message. The reply came after a long half hour that Allenford was too busy to see him. The Minister damned the arrogance of the man, but swallowing his pride, decided that in this instance the mountain must go to Mahomet. He went out into the panelled corridor, made his way down the Central lobby and across towards the Lord's chamber. Lord Allenford came out of the debate as he approached.

"Now look here, Allenford," he began angrily. Then he saw the scowl and tried flashing a smile. Both approaches fell on barren ground.

"Well?" said Allenford rudely. "I sent a message that I was busy. Didn't you get it?"

"Too busy to see a Minister of the Crown?" The Minister tried to keep his temper.

"I know what you're going to ask, and why waste both our times. You're busy too, I presume."

"You might at least have the courtesy to listen."

The two men stopped and stood facing each other in the middle of the broad passage. The walls, painted in the late nineteenth century with a battle scene from some forgotten phase of British history, in a style that the Minister had always thought was rather vulgar, served as a suitable backcloth for the minor battle developing in front. Lord Allenford, a large florid man with a loud and self-important voice, pushed back his jacket and placed his hands on his hips in an unpleasantly belligerent stance.

"Well?" he asked.

"You have a story of the Government's supposed involvement in Norsemen which, if released, would be of considerable embarrassment to us."

"I'm glad to have your independent confirmation of my own views. Your officials have already been pestering Tesco and my editors about it. That's why it hasn't come out so far. But it will, Minister, it will."

"We would like you to continue to withhold publication. It can do no good."

"It'll help my circulation, if nothing else," Allenford laughed unpleasantly.

"We wouldn't like to have to invoke the Official Secrets' Act."

"You wouldn't dare." Allenford knew he was right about that. The Minister was silent.

"In any case, the age of the Fourth Estate tycoon is dead, Minister," Allenford went on more helpfully. "You know that as well as I do. My newspapers are outpourings of machines. I've my hand on the helm, certainly I do, but so have a dozen others, and when it comes to content, it's the editors all the way. Even if I were to write something I'd be lucky to have it accepted. Business and journalism: strictly separate." The peer produced a large red and white spotted handkerchief and blew his nose loudly.

"So you won't help?"

"I'm not sure I want to. The truth will out."

"Do you want me to beg you?"

"I've had people on their knees before. It's most embarrassing to all concerned, I can assure you. So please don't indulge in histrionics, Minister. Quite simply, those of us in public positions shouldn't have things to hide. If this man Tesco has uncovered something and writes it, then you can prove it's not true. Or can you?" The peer's sharp eyes looked the Minister up and down. "Or can you?" he repeated.

"I'm not going to have my political future wrecked by some émigré middle-European gossip writer pretending to drag up non-existent dirt."

"Things on the career front surely aren't so rosy, since you turned down the Secretary of State's job and, if the dirt is non-existent, you've nothing to worry about, have you?" Allenford said unkindly. All of a sudden the peer's long-term dislike of the Minister began to show through more than a little. Some of his best friends were émigré middle-Europeans.

The Minister, realising he had gone too far, tried to change his tone.

"I'll be frank with you, Allenford," he began. The peer's eyes narrowed fractionally. When people said that they were going to be frank, it usually indicated something less than complete openness.

"I'll be frank. If things blow up, then it won't just be me who suffers. You must realise it would cause a major split in the party, and . . ."

"That's all right by me, Minister, quite all right. If it's ripe for a split who am I to hold it together? Now, if you will excuse me, I must be going." Without waiting for a response, Allenford turned rudely on his heel and walked away.

Had he glanced back, even Lord Allenford would have been surprised by the effect his words had produced. He might have wondered whether it could simply be anxiety over the prospect of the break-up of the party that had caused the Minister's face to turn ashen, or whether there must not be other, more personal reasons.

The Minister was standing motionless in the middle of the passage as if at a loss as to what to do next. Then, a few seconds later, a weak look of something less than despair crossed his face. Once again he had managed to come to terms with his own predicament. As always, he felt sure some global solution would emerge to the problem of Tesco and Allenford, which would, in the process, embrace the solution of his own very personal interest in suppressing publication.

He turned and walked slowly back along the corridor and into his own room. He would of course have to tell the P.M. about Allenford's attitude. Something could still be salvaged at that level without involving him further, but not tonight, no, not tonight. It was getting late and he had a long-standing engagement to fulfil.

When he pressed the buzzer on his desk, his Private Secretary came in at once.

"I've finished for today, Philip. You can put my papers away," the Minister said slowly. "There's no likelihood of any other crisis blowing up tonight, I hope?"

"No, Minister. Everything is fairly quiet for once. You *are* feeling all right, are you, Sir? You look a bit . . ."

"Quite all right, thank you." The Minister cut his P.S. short. "Quite all right," he repeated. "It's only that I'm afraid it was no go with Allenford, which is rather upsetting. It could be embarrassing. But that can damn well wait till tomorrow. He won't rush into print if I know him. Anyway I haven't time. I have a private dinner tonight and I don't want to be disturbed. You won't be able to get me on the phone. Oh, and I'll be late in tomorrow. I expect a fairly heavy night. Old school friends you know." He attempted to smile through the remnants of his worry.

The Private Secretary smiled politely back. He had his suspicions about some of the Minister's social activities, but nothing confirmed, nothing definite. And it was certainly no concern of a good Private Secretary, who should hear all and say little.

The Minister hadn't been lying. It *was* an old school friend of sorts who was taking him to the party. He had been promised a special and very discreet occasion that would be well worth the thirty pounds entry fee. Since his affair with Nicci was obviously coming to a rather unsatisfactory conclusion, he considered himself all the more in need of the relaxation, and the discretion alone was well worth the money. And if this particular festivity did leak out? Well, there might be a muted scandal and his wife would be upset, but it would blow over. She liked being a Minister's wife too much and she must know that Minister's morals couldn't always be above reproach. In any case, better this sort of scandal than a further one about the Norsemen.

He dined alone at the House, taking care not to drink too much. It tended to drown his sexual appetite and that would be rather a waste of his entry fee. He nurtured that part of his driving force as carefully as he did his political motivation and, in his view, it paid off on both accounts in the end. At one time he had been rather embarrassed by what he considered to be his over-concentration on sexual pursuits, but later discovered that most of his fellows had the same weakness, though only the lucky few had the prospect of putting their desires into a more high-flying practice than scruffy visits to "French Models" in Soho.

At ten o'clock precisely his old school friend was waiting for him in a Jaguar outside the House. A pale-faced, rather flabby man whom the Minister had never really liked even when he was a boy. But a man with contacts, a man on the fringes of everything who was a proven expert, at least, in his ability to organise special parties for his friends.

They drove northwards in silence to the palatial house in a discreet St. John's Wood avenue where the party was being held. It was already well under way when they arrived and before they were allowed in, their credentials were checked very carefully against a list by the rather severe-looking young man at the door. The Minister was offered a mask, and he gladly took the velvet cloth with the eye slits cut in it and put it on. He felt a bit eighteenth century wearing it, but he might decide to abandon it later if and when he felt more secure.

The hall lighting was subdued and the two men handed their coats to a stringy, topless waitress who smilingly offered them drinks in return. The Minister remarked that the welcome was a little obvious and hoped that it became a fraction more subtle later. His friend said nothing but led him through into a large drawing room where the main action seemed to be taking place. The atmosphere was already pretty uninhibited. There were perhaps twenty people scattered around the room in various states of dress, the girls prettier and rather more lightly clad than their more elderly, prosperous, and as yet more constrained male partners, for whose benefit the party was being expensively provided.

A floor show or, more precisely, a mattress show was warming up, amid a pile of cushions, in the centre of the room. There seemed to be at least three bodies frenetically entwined in the act. The Minister stood uncertainly in the half-light for a moment or so and then took a back seat on a low sofa in a darkened corner. His friend had disappeared.

He had hardly settled down to watch the writhings when two quite well-endowed girls, one tall with long blonde hair, the other dark and petite came up and sat down uninvited one on either side of him. He smiled at them in nervous anticipation of what was to come.

SEVENTEEN

Oslo, Tuesday Afternoon

Walt Tesco was beginning to enjoy himself. After the pain and unpleasantness of his encounter with the skinheads, it was all very gratifying the way things had begun to hang together. Only twenty-four hours in Oslo and three days since Rossetti's story had set him on his way, and he already knew all about the fire at the big house in the suburbs. He had been told of the tragic death of the owner, a man called Schoeyen, and about his strangely capable house guest, a large man, said to be a doctor, who had been much in evidence.

With the help of a Norwegian journalist colleague, he had driven up that morning to interview some foresters working near where the house had stood. They had seen two of the survivors, both suffering from severe shock and exposure, taken away by the doctor and his friends, carried on stretchers from their hut in the forest. No one knew where they had gone. As luck would have it, and just as Tesco was leaving the site of the fire, one of the workers had pointed to a woman approaching them up the drive. That was the former housekeeper, the man said. A formidable woman, and to avoid trouble they'd better get out of her way, unless, of course, Mr. Tesco wanted to talk to her.

Tesco didn't, and they passed her on their way out, ignoring her suspicious, hostile looks. Tesco had thanked both the woodmen and his journalist colleague and left them, saying he was going back to the centre of town. Once out of their sight however, he had waited in the trees by his hired car, watching the woman till she too had left. He followed her.

So that was why at that moment he was sitting at one of the cubicled tables in the *Teater Café*, just across the road from the National Theatre in central Oslo. His quarry was sitting nearby, a coffee and an open sandwich in front of her. Tesco could easily keep her in view without being seen. He ordered himself a beer and something to eat as well and settled down to wait until she decided to move again. He surveyed the restaurant contentedly. It was the sort of genuinely old-fashioned atmosphere that he enjoyed, full of memories of Ibsen and of Norwegian literary and artistic life at the turn of the century. Caricatures and drawings of people of the age hung around the walls, adding to the ambience. Up above was a sort of incongruous minstrel gallery where, despite the earliness of the hour, an elderly pianist and a man with a violin were already playing romantic music of the Grand Hotel variety.

The woman was waiting for someone. She kept glancing irritably at her watch and looking towards the door. After about a quarter of an hour a man came in. He sat down beside her, picked up a menu card and made to order something for himself. But the woman was standing now, angrily pointing at her watch. Her loud voice carried easily across to Tesco, but though he spoke no Norwegian and her precise words were lost on him, the message was clear enough. The woman was late for something, the man shrugged resignedly, and they both got up and left the restaurant.

Tesco followed them into the street and down the busy street towards the harbour. They were making for one of the ferry boats that connected the centre of the capital with some of the more outlying suburbs dotted along the Oslofjord. He went on board just behind them, straining his ears to catch where they were buying their tickets to. Despite the unfamiliar language he thought he recognised the name of one of the villages on the route and asked for a ticket to the same place. He appreciated it was a long shot, this tail on the woman. She might well be staying separately after the fire, but judging from the size of the house that had burned down, her employer would have been able to afford, in common with most of his neighbours, to have a country house somewhere by the fjord.

They had got on board just in time. The boat's engine roared to life before Tesco was properly in his seat. He placed himself behind the woman, taking care to hide his face behind his newspaper every time she looked in his direction, just in case she might recognise him from the morning's brief encounter. The ferry pulled powerfully away from the quay, causing the water to boil as it gathered speed. Tesco relaxed and sat back to enjoy the ride. The fjord, fresh and sparkling in the spring sunshine, was framed by the hills behind, still under their covering of snow.

He gazed out at the foam on the fast-flowing water and reviewed the situation. That there was evidence, provided by Rossetti, of a rather sensational leak in London had, for the moment, receded into the background. The immediate question was what had happened to the girl and to MacCaig. The foresters' story of their suffering from shock and exposure seemed too facile and there must be more behind it. The conclusion at best was that they were being held against their will; at worst . . . ? And what did it all hold out for him? Why had he, Walt Tesco, come gallivanting over to Oslo in the first place? A story certainly, which, with the evidence already provided by that gilded ass of a civil servant last Saturday night, would build into a very nice scandal story. He allowed himself a momentary dream of fame. The press lords of Fleet Street would fall over themselves for the exclusive rights and, though he was to a certain extent now committed to Lord Allenford's paper, he was still his own master, especially if that particular baron succumbed to Government pressure not to publish. He had plenty of other markets. But he also had to admit that there was a weaker side to his hard-bitten journalistic front. He was just a trifle romantic, and a girl in distress was always appealing.

He sat up with a start. The ferry had reduced speed and was gliding slowly in towards a little pier. The woman and her companion were preparing to disembark. Above the sound of the engine Tesco could hear her irritated complaints, presumably still about having been kept late. He got up to follow them.

On shore, the pier led up to a cluster of gaily painted wooden houses, a couple of shops, and a clean-looking hotel. A black Volvo was parked alone in the little square in front. The two walked quickly across to it, got in and drove off down the long road which ran along the shore away from the square. Tesco stopped in his tracks and looked round frustratedly for some way of following them. Then, as the car turned a corner by a headland and was lost to view, he shrugged resignedly and advanced on the hotel. In a small community it would be unusual if he didn't find someone who would be willing to talk.

Chelsea, Tuesday Evening

The Minister had been delayed by having to hang about and vote at the House. It had reached a highly critical clause of the new Prices and Incomes Bill and there was a Three-Line Whip on. Then he had had some tidying up to do after the P.M. had successfully dragooned Lord Allenford into delaying letting the cat out of the bag, and afterwards, unable to find the driver of his official Humber, he had had to take a taxi. So he was hardly in an amiable mood when he arrived at the house in Pont Street. Everyone was in evening dress, and from the waiters in white monkey-jackets circling the table, the sparkling silverware, the range of crystal glasses by each place, to the glint of a discreet tiara on the hostess's head, the scene was very much of elegant high society at its best. The Minister, having taken some years to gain and retain entry to such society, now openly enjoyed it and the prospect of a glittering evening did much to restore him to immediate good temper.

His hostess hadn't held up her dinner party and the other guests were already seated round the candlelit dinner table, well advanced with the first course. Conversation was animated, but there was a sudden hush as he was shown into the dining room and his host and hostess came up to greet him. He had the momentary feeling that he had just ceased being the subject of discussion, but it flattered rather than worried him.

Apologising profusely, he took the guest of honour's place on the right of his hostess. Only then did he begin to focus properly on the other guests. Some he recognised as members of the usual gilded set he would have expected to find at this particular house. But there was another.

"And you know Stefan Issouna of old, I understand, Minister."

His hostess was talking to him and he forced himself to smile through the shock of recognising the man sitting opposite him.

"Stefan had been telling us of the times you used to have together—you naughty man."

"What . . .?" the Minister began palely. Stefan surely couldn't have been talking.

"I've just been describing our nights on the town in Copenhagen, Minister—no secrets, of course—just the junketing." The large, glistening face of the man opposite split in a leaden smile of reassurance, and the Minister relaxed a little.

"I really *do* think you two have something to hide," chirruped the hostess. "You looked quite worried for an instant, Minister."

"Not at all. Not at all. Delighted to see you again, Stefan. What a wonderful surprise. What are you doing here, and why didn't you let me know you were coming?" The Minister spoke a fraction too quickly. Anyone who knew him well would have seen the nervous strain.

The big man replied slowly with some elaborate pun about coming to study Parkinson's disease in Whitehall. Everyone laughed. He produced a white silk handkerchief and began patting methodically at his brow. The Minister stared fascinatedly like a rabbit at a snake. He remembered that gesture only too well.

The memory of Copenhagen in the long hot summer of 1956, *and a year begun as a brilliant language student, drawing to its disastrous culmination. A year of beautiful, too-willing girls, of swimming, sailing and merely living in a town that he enjoyed for its freshness and its freedoms. Nights playing and drinking in the Tivoli pleasure gardens; days cruising among the Danish islands, where at the beginning, in his memory if not in fact, the sun had shone endlessly. But the clouds of involvement had rolled in too soon. The attractions of the extreme nationalism had proved strong and the student had been quickly drawn into the network of a neo-fascist political group. Internationally based, with funds drawn from dubious former Axis funds, he had revelled in the excitement of conspiracy. Later, but too late, he had seen the naïvety and the dangers of fascism and had swung well to the left.*

But before that stage had been reached there had been the demonstration. A meeting of his group had been attacked in its coffee-bar committee room by a group of young communists. He had escaped the worst of the resultant fight and had been making his way out through a back entrance of the café into a side street. A young communist student had appeared, unexpectedly blocking his way, shouting foul abuse. In self-defence, he claimed, he had seized a piece of scrap metal piping and had struck and struck and struck. . . .

Stefan Issouna had arrived, fortuitously, unexpected as always, as the sole witness. Stefan the diplomat; Stefan the mystery; above all, Stefan the professional political agitator with whom he had talked often, long and late. Slightly perspiring, caressing his forehead with a white silk handkerchief, Stefan had understood, realised, known what to do, while he had stood dazed and shuddering. It had all been so simple, the body dragged to the roof-top, the gin poured over the clothes and into the dead mouth, the push, the sickening thud clearly audible even from that height.

Stefan Issouna, the body, Copenhagen that summer had all receded with a growing ability to find peace of mind after unpleasantness. Nearly seven years and he had met Stefan Issouna again, by chance, in Piccadilly. Surprised and delighted that by this time the student had become an M.P., Stefan had given him dinner a few days later—dinner and a chance piece of information that allowed him to ask an innocent question in the House about defence costs. The subsequent political scandal made the young M.P.'s name famous, and he had, in consequence, further reason to be grateful to Stefan.

There had been no unpleasantness, no persuasion or pressure, but the M.P. had been helpful in a number of ways since then, when Stefan had difficulties. Getting an alien into the country by lobbying the Home Office, asking the odd embarrassingly well-informed question, which led to a change in government policy. All above board and straight, and that summer in Copenhagen was never mentioned.

Then, as a Junior Minister, Stefan had asked one question too many and had been refused. He had merely shrugged, wiped the shine off his brow, looked slightly hurt and disappeared for a few days. Then he came back and asked the same question as if he had never been refused. There was a threat of stirring deep waters, and the Minister had taken the easy way out. It hadn't seemed very important information at the time. Since then, Stefan had come back once or perhaps twice every six months, never pressing his luck, never going too far in cornering the Minister, but always asking for a little more and with a little more persistence. The Minister had grown to fear these visitations from the man with the white silk handkerchief. It disturbed his even progress towards success and there was a limit to what he could conveniently pigeon-hole and forget in the recesses of his memory. That had been the case when he did what he was told and had passed on what he knew of MacCaig's projected mission against the Norsemen. His information on that had been premature, but his officials simply hadn't told him that MacCaig had only been named for the job and was recuperating in Scotland. But what else could he have done? In any case that incident didn't matter, since everyone now seemed to assume they could only have known about MacCaig through the stolen files, despite the evidence of the visitors to his uncle's farm. But then there was also a vague, uneasy feeling that something he had once said casually to Stefan might have led to the murder of the agent in Oslo; again there was the phone call about MacCaig and the girl; there was the Tesco affair. Now things were accelerating. He closed his mind with a snap. He knew that to think about it could bring him close to madness.

The rest of the dinner was a troubled blur for the Minister. He was fortunate in having an elderly peeress on his right who did all the talking and who took her considerable opportunity of letting him have predictable opinions of the demerits of the present government. He reacted with Pavlovian ability, appearing to be listening intently without doing so. His mind was firmly elsewhere.

Stefan couldn't be there by chance. He was never anywhere

by chance; everything he did was carefully planned and programmed, and the Minister knew that he would have come with some query or demand once again. He fought down a panic, and, to compensate, drank too much wine. By the time the ladies withdrew and his immediate neighbour had removed the protection of her ability to talk non-stop, he was drunk.

The men, left at the table with their brandy and cigars, paired into groups and he was inevitably drawn to Stefan. He braced himself.

"How are you, my dear chap?" Stefan asked. The opener on its own spelled out the dangers. Stefan Issouna had never indulged in small talk and his use of the word "chap", with only the very slightest trace of an accent, jarred its own warning signal.

"What are you doing here?" the Minister whispered fiercely. "Don't you realise how dangerous it is?"

"Talking to Ministers of the Crown is surely safe enough. I understand that, under your system, your Prime Minister has to give his personal authority before Ministers are followed and watched, and he would hardly suspect you—you in your position."

"What do you want?"

"Must I want something?" The heavy face split mirthlessly. "But you're right, of course. It's just co-operation I look for, as always. You know how it is." The white silk handkerchief was extracted and applied once again. "I find it extremely close in here, don't you? Now that the British have discovered central heating, they'll have to learn how to regulate it. But you're perspiring too. Come, come, Minister, you must relax. You've helped us a great deal, and with the two in Oslo on ice, things generally are under control."

"That journalist Tesco, whom in an unfortunate moment your Government called on to discredit us, has, thanks to both our efforts and I understand to that of your Prime Minister when he spoke to Allenford, had his story suppressed. We have to keep it that way until Norsemen proper gets under way. To do so, we need more positive assistance from you. We have an action programme which, at the British end, you are in a very good position to organise. Certain acts of a, shall we say, drastic nature, violent if you prefer it, have to be carried through to create the uncertainty and fear necessary for our further . . ."

The Minister, strengthened by the drink, drew in a short breath and went very pale. "No," he hissed.

"No, what?" the other man asked gently. "I haven't explained anything yet."

"The answer is still no. What happened to the two who went to Oslo whom I telephoned about? What did you mean when you said they were on ice? You haven't . . . You haven't . . .?"

"Are they on your conscience, Minister? They might well be. They are safe, and hostages to your co-operation. Just as are the files you helped us steal."

"I never helped you steal any files."

"Of course you did. You called your man Rossetti over at the appropriate time, didn't you? How else could we have got them."

The Minister looked puzzled for a moment. The drink was beginning to tell heavily on him. He took a balloon glass of brandy from the table in front of him and drank deeply. "No," he said fiercely. "And the files—I don't know what you're talking about. No, no, no," he repeated.

"Then let's not waste time talking further. Surely it's time to join the ladies." Issouna smiled, wiped his face with the back of his hand, turned slowly round in his chair and began speaking pointedly to his host.

EIGHTEEN

Oslo, Wednesday Morning

"I hope she's keeping strictly to her instructions," whispered MacCaig. "Can you hear that old clock chiming away outside somewhere? I make it quarter past eleven now and if she's sticking to the seven-hour injection schedule, then we've still got a clear three-quarters of an hour to play with."

"Why did that man misjudge?" Fiona Ross whispered back. "He said he was a doctor."

"He said he used to be a doctor—different thing altogether. He needs a refresher course since he should have realised that we would need progressively stronger doses. It's several days now and we're becoming immune to whatever the dope is they're pumping us with."

"I hardly feel immune. I can scarcely move and I've a headache like fifty hangovers."

"Take it slowly." MacCaig raised himself slowly in the bed and looked cautiously about him, staring curiously at the clinically white surroundings of his prison, looking for some inspiration for future action. "Wriggle your toes and fingers as much as you can. I don't know much about this sort of thing, but it should help burn the stuff out of the system a little quicker."

"Wriggling toes isn't going to get us out of here."

"Behind these chintz curtains there are bars on the window. That's as far as I can see. I'm going to have a look." MacCaig swung the quilt back from his bed and attempted to put his legs out on to the floor. To his surprise, he was dressed in a pair of quite respectable pyjamas, but his own clothes were nowhere to be seen. He tried to struggle to a vertical position and by the time he had succeeded, he was pouring with sweat. "Well, one thing's certain, Issouna isn't back yet," he said gasping.

"How d'you know?"

"Feel how warm it is? He'd have the heating turned down the moment he came in the door. Remember how sensitive he is. It must be something to do with his size that he sweats so much." MacCaig smiled reassuringly in her direction. "When he's put on trial, I'll bet his defence lawyer will plead that his disability turned him to crime."

"*Please*, Calder. Don't fool. I can't stand much more of this."

"Sorry, Fiona, but look. I'm more or less on my feet." He felt very faint and his legs were like lead weights, but he tried to keep sounding cheerful. He pushed himself boldly off the bed and immediately collapsed in a heap on the floor. There was a considerable crash.

"Calder, are you all right?"

"Lie still," he whispered back urgently. "If she comes, I'll play unconscious."

They waited motionless for a couple of minutes but no one appeared. MacCaig risked trying to get to his feet again. The fall seemed to have done him some good, and he felt a little more alert. He crawled slowly towards the window, slipping on the polished wooden floor as he went. Eventually he made it and reached up to the sill to look out.

They were in the basement of what seemed a fairly large house, with the bottom of the window on a level with the ground. There was a rock-strewn garden of sorts, still covered with snow, pine trees everywhere, and the ground seemed to slope sharply away in front, presumably down to the shore. The sound of waves on rocks was continuous and loud.

Straining his head, MacCaig could see a man cleaning a black Volvo to the side of the house. The man turned from his task and MacCaig heard voices. Then the housekeeper appeared. She was standing just in front of the window, a laundry basket in her hand. The whole scene looked so domestic and normal.

"What's happening," Fiona asked. He told her, drawing back a little to avoid being seen.

"There seems to be only the two of them about, but one never knows. I'm going to try the door."

"Can't you wait a little, you're not fit."

A bell rang in the recesses of the house. MacCaig heard the sound of footsteps above, and the woman's voice raised in enquiry. Somehow he struggled back to the bed and pulled the quilt over him. But again after a moment or so, when no one had appeared, he got out once more.

"I'm going to risk it," he said.

"Risk what?"

"We've got to get a message out. There's not much time."

"You can't leave me here."

"After we get out of here I promise you I won't ever leave you again. You won't get rid of me even if you want to. But now I must. I won't be long." Through the strain she saw real affection in his eyes for the first time. She smiled encouragement back at him.

MacCaig crawled softly towards the door. Just as he reached it he saw to his horror that the handle was turning very slowly. With supreme effort he stood up and moved silently behind the door as it opened inwards. As he went, he picked up the pottery jug, which was standing on a little side table by the wall, and raised it above his head as a weapon, struggling to keep it gripped in his still very weak hands.

The door opened slowly and cautiously. MacCaig knew that if whoever it was didn't come in quickly, he would both have to drop the jug and fall himself. After what seemed like an age, a head appeared within his line of vision. He started to bring the heavy jug down.

"No," Fiona hissed urgently. "No, it's a friend, Calder."

Walt Tesco, despite his utterly unathletic bulk, came into the room and easily managed to reach up and disarm the bewildered MacCaig. Then, seeing that something was drastically the matter, helped the other man back over to the bed.

"What is it?" said Tesco, with a display of remarkable control.

"Some sort of drug," said Fiona briefly.

"Aha," said Tesco wisely. Then he turned and went cautiously back to the door and looked out. "Still undiscovered," he muttered almost to himself. He shut the door quietly.

"Would you mind telling me who the hell this is," gasped MacCaig, looking oddly at Fiona.

"He's a journalist, I think, Mr . . ."

"Tesco. . . . Walt Tesco. Pleased to meet you." Tesco extended a hand automatically and then withdrew it at once. "Sorry, it's a habit. This is hardly the place for formalities."

"What are you doing here?" asked Fiona.

"Looking for a story, and for you, of course," he added as an afterthought. He beamed myopically through his thick pebble lenses.

"But how?"

"Questions, if I may suggest, could wait. We have to get you out, and it may not be too easy."

"Don't they know you're here."

"Certainly not. I rang the door bell and ran away like a schoolboy. While they were working out how it had happened, I slipped in the back way."

"How many are there?" MacCaig asked. He had managed to regain a little of his composure.

"I only saw two, a man and a woman."

A clock struck in the background.

"That's quarter to twelve," said Fiona quietly.

"So?" asked Tesco.

"They'll be coming any minute to give us another jab, that's all."

Tesco tutted to himself under his breath. He disliked the prospect of violence. "If time's that short, then I should disappear and muster some help. Even if you were to get another jab, I assume you'd be safe enough till I return?" He looked swiftly at them to gauge their reactions to his suggestion. Fiona shivered involuntarily and looked at MacCaig. He shook his head slowly.

"It's not on. Even if you get away, it will take you a while to get people organised. This is Wednesday, isn't it, and they're expecting their boss back anytime. When he comes I don't think we should be here, for a number of obvious reasons."

Tesco looked worried, then shrugged. "By 'their boss' I suppose you mean this doctor. Well, whatever you say," he replied slowly. "Now let me see. You're not very agile, so I think I'd at least better go and find some transport as a first step." As he spoke, he turned towards the door, opened it, and immediately came face to face with the startled housekeeper who was standing outside, a cloth-covered tray in her hands.

It would have been hard to judge which of them was the more surprised, but remarkably, Tesco took the initiative. He reached forward, grabbed her by her white coat and dragged her bodily into the room. The door slammed shut behind them partially drowning her angry shout.

Fiona was rather confused by what happened next. She herself made a vain attempt to get up and assist in some way, but found her limbs still totally refused to support her, so she remained sitting up in her bed, a helpless spectator of the scene. Tesco had ended up on the floor, more or less seated on top of the struggling woman. He was holding one of her arms behind her in a professional-looking lock and at the same time was trying to gag her with a towel she had been carrying, in an attempt to stifle her shouts. In the turmoil, his thick-lensed glasses had been knocked off and they were lying broken in a corner of the room. His eyes were swollen and screwed up as he tried to make out what was going on around him.

MacCaig meanwhile had risen and crawled across towards the door. Fiona could see him picking something up from the floor and advancing on the struggling pair. It was a chrome hypodermic syringe—already loaded for use on them. Together the two men held the housekeeper and MacCaig shakily inserted the needle in her arm. A minute or so passed, and the woman's struggles and muffled shouts gradually grew fainter.

"O.K. Well done. You can get off now," said MacCaig breathlessly. He watched with a grudging flicker of admiration, as the fat little man climbed helplessly to his feet knocking against a table in the process. Tesco was very obviously almost blind without his spectacles.

"Have you seen my glasses?" he said plaintively.

"Here they are—badly broken I'm afraid, though one lens may be usable."

Tesco took the shattered frames and tried to balance them on his nose. He peered about him through one of the lenses and then grinned happily. "Could have been worse. I have a spare pair at the hotel. Now, what about her?" He looked down in a businesslike way at the inert body at his feet.

"Into the bed with her if you can manage on your own. I'm not much use yet. Take off her white coat and her shoes. We may need them. Quickly. Her friend hasn't turned up yet but he may do at any moment."

They dragged the housekeeper over to the bed and Tesco threw her on it, covering her over with the quilt. To a casual observer it would now seem like one of them lying there.

"Right now. This time I think we'd better go together," said MacCaig firmly. He was standing now, still shaky but feeling much more able after his exertions. "Fiona, you take the white coat and the shoes until we find our clothes or something else that fits. We'll dress up the other bed with pillows, schoolboy-style and make it look like a second body."

They did this quickly and then the three of them prepared to leave—Tesco helping Fiona up and taking the brunt of her weight on his shoulders, despite his own semi-blindness. MacCaig came limping drunkenly behind, full of wonder at the other man's resilience.

Out into a wood-panelled hall and over towards some stairs leading to the ground floor. Still no sign of the other man. They started to climb up—a considerable effort for each of them. Just as they reached the landing, and out of sight, there was a noise below them. The man had come in to the cellar, presumably through another door. The three froze into silence and listened while he went in to the room they had just vacated. He obviously spotted nothing amiss for he came out immediately and went on about his business. They heard him clattering about below with buckets and brushes.

Stealthily the three continued on their way. They came to the main hall and there was the front door, with, parked outside, the black Volvo. Only a few more paces to freedom.

Still there was no appearance by the man. They knew that in their weak state and with Tesco almost blinded, their chances would be slim, especially if he had a weapon. On top of it all, when they made the open, Fiona and MacCaig began shivering violently in the bitter cold after their days of confinement in bed. They had hardly anything to cover themselves and had no time to waste in further search.

Tesco put his coat round Fiona and brought her to the car. The man had been washing it and a bunch of keys still hung from the ignition. Tesco helped the girl into the front and turned round enquiringly.

"D'you think you can drive?" MacCaig asked him. "I don't think I have the strength."

Tesco nodded slowly and got into the driving seat while MacCaig clambered in behind.

"I'm pretty useless and have never actually passed a test," said Tesco happily. "And that was with glasses. You'll tell me when we come to a corner? Now where are the keys?"

"For God's sake hurry. They're in the ignition," barked MacCaig, his self-control going for the first time.

Tesco found the switch and then lost the gear lever. Fiona indicated the automatic clutch to him and after what seemed an age, Tesco, protesting his total ignorance of a system of driving without a gear stick, managed to get the car going.

"Teamwork," he said proudly, as the car lurched drunkenly forward. "You British are wonderful. It's all so easy. . . ."

At that moment a shot rang out from the house, and then another. The glass in the rear window shattered and Tesco seemed to jerk peculiarly in his seat. But he kept hold of the wheel, almost leaning on it as he peered blindly in front of him. Glancing backwards, through the gap in the broken glass, MacCaig saw the man standing in the middle of the drive, firing rapidly in their direction but he was obviously inexpert and no other shots hit the car. Then he appeared to run out of bullets for he threw the gun down in the snow, turned and hurried into the house.

"Gone to telephone for reinforcements. But we're well away," MacCaig said in a relaxed voice, as he turned back in his seat to look the way they were going. He stiffened as he saw the blood on the back of Tesco's jacket. They were travelling very fast down a narrow road by the shore. Fiona was leaning over, helping Tesco hold the wheel.

"Are you all right?" MacCaig asked naïvely.

"Got to keep going," Tesco muttered. "Keep low, they're coming."

"Who is?"

"Look behind you. You'll see."

MacCaig turned. A large Mercedes had appeared from nowhere and was advancing on them, easily catching up. In a moment it was alongside them forcing them into the side of the road. Tesco lost his grip and slipped sideways from the wheel into Fiona's lap, his foot fortunately coming off the accelerator as he did so. MacCaig tried to reach over to grab the wheel, but as he moved, the Volvo skidded on a patch of ice, turned round and into a bank of snow piled by the roadside, and came to a grinding halt in the side of the now stationary Mercedes.

The two young police officers from the Mercedes managed to force open the Volvo's off-side door and one of them shouted something in Norwegian in the direction of the re-emerging figure of Tesco. MacCaig caught the sense of the remark.

"They're arresting you for speeding and on suspicion of being drunk in charge," he said. Then he lay back in the rear seat, closed his eyes and began laughing gently to himself.

NINETEEN

The Great North Road, Wednesday Night

The Minister sat back comfortably in the rear seat. It was one of the greatest pleasures of rank, being driven everywhere. This was especially true late at night when, like now, it was raining heavily. The glare of passing car headlights on the wet road added to the comfort inside the Humber. He leaned forward and shut the sliding glass partition between himself and the driver, and then, sitting well back in the leather seat, he closed his eyes. He could almost forget.

He would never permit himself to think of what he was doing as evil. It was a simple matter of self-preservation—something which every politician had recourse to from time to time. Admittedly here it was more extreme, but, once conveniently put in perspective, had he really acted so differently from how others would have done? He comforted himself with the negative. Everyone had a part of their past which they wished to forget about, if not to hide. This evening's work would soon become part of that past which could be gently nudged into untouched memory—like Copenhagen that summer.

Almost untroubled by the essence of what he had just done, he was angry nonetheless at his own behaviour, for a different reason. Stefan had come back to repeat his demand made at the dinner-table. This time he hadn't been fortified with drink. He had been weak and had once again allowed himself to be bullied. That mustn't happen again. He would have to formulate a contingency plan for the next time Stefan came into focus. He was alive enough to the dangers to realise that, like with a spoilt child, something given in the long run encouraged an ever-increasing demand for more. Perhaps he really would leave, quit politics for a field where pasts didn't matter so much, where threats and blackmail—that was a word he hadn't used before—wouldn't work. He could resign, but his sheet would have to be clean and honourable when he did so. It was all a matter of timing.

The Humber's tyres screeched suddenly on the wet road as the driver tried to avoid a lightless cyclist. For a moment the Minister was brought back from his thoughts in a panic of physical fear. But there was no accident and the driver accelerated once again.

The Minister leant forward, opened the glass partition and muttered a few words of understanding about yokels without traffic sense, to the obviously incensed driver. Then he sat back again in his seat. He was pouring with sweat.

He forced himself back to his thoughts. Now he realised how much there was in the political life that he hated, circumstances such as the one where the P.M. could force him into taking over a job with which he had no sympathy. He had been forced. But was that the real reasons as opposed to a mere excuse?

And back to Stefan. Three or was it four times now he had acted for Stefan over the Norsemen. Setting aside the worry that he might in some way be responsible for the death under the grenade in Oslo, in the first real instance he had merely passed on MacCaig's name believing he was already in charge of eliminating the Norsemen. That project had misfired, but then that civil servant Rossetti had been beaten up and robbed. It too hadn't mattered much, but nonetheless he had been shocked at the brutality. Stefan had said he had helped there, but that wasn't true. And the Tesco affair? There he had been acting for the State as well. The Government had, for political reasons, wanted the story suppressed, and the P.M. himself had succeeded in buying Allenford off. The next time—the telephone call—what had that indicated? What had Stefan meant about the two in Oslo being "on ice"? He mustn't be allowed to kill them.

But MacCaig was paid for doing his job. He was dedicated and cold. The dinner that night at the Club had proven that well enough. He had started to look for help from MacCaig, but it hadn't worked. He had hoped for some way out of his link with Stefan and the past. He had almost told him, but then MacCaig had mentioned that it had been his friend Tinker under that grenade in the snow. The bitterness had frozen the rest of the evening. The Minister knew from that moment on that he had to find his own salvation and, in consequence, Stefan must do whatever he had to do. But there was the girl as well—Fiona Ross. That was different.

Again he thought what else he could have done. A twinge of remorse, of anxiety, of something deeper, ran briefly through him. He gazed out at the darkness and at the rain on the windows, searching for help. Then he resigned himself to the fact that he would telephone Stefan again tomorrow and plead gentleness, promising to do what Stefan asked of him in return. It was a matter of life or death. He was being forced. Eventually he *must* find a way out of the circle. The Royal Commission idea might help.

The facile thought eased his conscience sufficiently and he slept.

Chelsea, Thursday Morning

Rossetti lay on his bed wrapped in a beautiful shot-silk dressing gown. One manicured hand held a cup of weak china tea; the other, the morning's copy of *The Times*. He read the lobby correspondent's report with remarkable detachment.

His bedroom, like the rest of his apartment, was decorated in a style that was far from spartan. Everything was in the best of current good taste, from the modern paintings on the walls to the colour and texture of the well-cut curtains. A mixture, delicately blended, of antique pieces of furniture and modern items of convenience and comfort, displaying, as its only fault, an inclination to femininity which was out of keeping with the totally bachelor circumstances. It was a bedroom created and assembled with genuine expertise as well as with a great deal of money. And Rossetti had both.

He placed his cup precisely back in its saucer on the marble-topped bedside table, and, stretching lengthwise against the large pile of silk covered pillows, grasped *The Times* more capably in both hands. He read on.

In the face of growing clamour, the P.M. with typical British compromise had decided to take the bull by the horns or whatever, and was setting up a Royal Commission to investigate federalist demands for broader political groupings in Northern Europe. That, thought Rossetti as he took a sip of tea, would effectively bury organisations like the Norsemen for quite a few years, or at least, until the Report came out. It was an old, worn trick which would be recognised as such, but would work nonetheless. The Minister was to be nominated Chairman of the Commission. The lobby correspondent's normally reliable sources couldn't be sure, but rumour in Westminster circles had it that the Minister might give up all his other duties in favour of devoting himself fully to the work of the new Commission.

Rossetti sighed. Things weren't going quite according to plan, and not everyone would be pleased. But he had done his best. That was the trouble with getting involved; all these horrid subjective judgments. He had heard nothing further from that revolting man Tesco, and hoped that nothing more embarrassing would arise on that front. The Minister had been compromised, that was the main thing. But the compromising had come from him, and if Tesco by chance re-emerged, the finger of blame could be pointed at him and difficult questions might be asked. He had better indulge in a little more gossiping around. It served to blur the trail, for if a lot of people knew from a variety of sources, there was less chance of his being found out as the original culprit. And Rossetti had his own future to think about. Languidly he pulled himself up on his bank of pillows and poured himself another cup of tea. In a minute or so he would have to summon up enough energy to get up and face the day.

Then the buzzer at the door of his flat went. He sighed again and laid *The Times* down on the quilt. Life was such a strain.

His housekeeper hadn't arrived yet so he'd have to deal with the post or the milk or the laundry himself. He eased himself to his feet and went to the door.

There were three of them standing in the entrance. He recognised the two men but not the girl, but even in his surprise he realised who she must be. Tesco had his arm in a sling.

"Yes, do come in. I'm afraid you've caught me . . ." he began. But they were already through into the large living room, MacCaig leading the way.

Having slightly regained his composure, Rossetti started to say something cutting about the rudeness of their intrusion, but the tenseness of their looks stopped him. For once he waited in silence.

"Right now, Rossetti," MacCaig said abruptly, seating himself down unasked in an armchair. "Just repeat what you told our friend Mr. Tesco here in the pub the other night."

"Oh my God," said Rossetti. He turned to look accusingly at Tesco. "You promised you wouldn't. Now I've had it, especially after what's in the papers. My career will be ruined. The Minister will at best sue for libel."

"Come on now. Stop gabbling and make it snappy," said MacCaig. "There's not much time."

"I'd like my lawyer present," Rossetti replied with a show of nerves. That was the thing to ask for in such circumstances.

"Perhaps I'd better explain," said Tesco a fraction more kindly. "We're all rather tired, having just returned from Oslo, and we think there may not be too much time to lose."

"I don't understand," said Rossetti. It appeared all too much for him. He sat down shakily.

Tesco, despite MacCaig's protestations that he was wasting his effort, quietly explained what had happened, believing that without some of the background Rossetti couldn't be expected to co-operate. He told Rossetti about the capture and the rescue and about how the Norwegian police were now tidying up the pieces back in Oslo. They had arrested the woman housekeeper and a couple of the men. One of them under interrogation had given a few hints about Issouna's present whereabouts and as to who his contact in London had been. All the signs pointed to the Minister.

So Rossetti had been right. There was nothing to fear. Rossetti had done well, Tesco said.

Rossetti smiled weakly. MacCaig was talking to him again. He was asking him to go and see the Minister, drop a few hints about what he had discovered, and see how the man reacted. The idea was to get the Minister to give himself away, to get him to panic, and with luck also to get him to show the way to where Issouna was.

"But I couldn't. I couldn't possibly. I want to stay *right* out of it. Besides it might be dangerous. The Minister will be desperate. He might do anything, anything." Rossetti started to protest.

MacCaig was standing now. He went across and angrily gripped the lapels of Rossetti's dressing gown. He started to shake him, shouting at him that he had to do what he was told or else. Rossetti appeared quite frightened. Then Tesco was gently pulling them apart, and while Fiona Ross got MacCaig to relax, Tesco achieved, by persuasion, what he believed more violent methods would never have done.

Tesco smiled sweetly while he told the shivering man that unless he did as he was told, the fact that Rossetti had suppressed the evidence, except to tell a gossip journalist, would become widely known. It was too late to start covering up and the choice was clear.

Park Lane, Thursday Evening

The scene in the foyer of the Hilton was rather like a high society version of Waterloo Station in the rush hour. A petty Emir from the Gulf made his stately way through the curious throng followed by a strong retinue of wives and advisers. A group of noisy, sun-tanned American tourists were querulously attempting to book-in, and a strikingly beautiful starlet surrounded by about a dozen reporters was just leaving for Biarritz. The lead, which attached her to one of her three poodles, caught round the legs of her bored but equally beautiful male companion, and the subsequent prima-donna anger had the photographers' flash-lights popping away joyfully for their gossip columns.

The Minister slipped almost unnoticed through the crowd towards the row of phone cubicles at the far side of the hall. One of the assistant hotel detectives, who was loitering discreetly by the news-stand, recognised him briefly and then looked away. Junior Ministers were commonplace at the Hilton.

The Minister walked quickly. He had given considerable thought to where he should make the call. The Oslo line was, he presumed, still being tapped so he couldn't risk phoning from his home, office or club. But he had to get through, to urge Stefan to be kind, ask him for help in return for his co-operation. With any luck there would be a delay in the call being traced. He had to risk it and there wasn't much time.

Was it his imagination that the operator's voice became strangely alert after he gave her the Oslo number? "There is some delay," she said. "Could you hold on please." He glanced at his watch and stared anxiously out of the window of the cubicle at the milling scrum of hotel guests.

A couple of minutes passed. The operator spoke again, "It appears the line is out of order. The subscriber's house has been damaged by fire, we understand. But please hold on. We've been given an alternative number, and I'm trying that now."

A warning light went on inside the Minister's brain. "House damaged by fire." Odd that the operator should know such details. Lines were either working or out of order. Unless this particular line was being talked about. The girl's voice came back on the line. "I'm having some difficulty, caller. Where're you ringing from. . .? Hello. Caller. . . . Hello?"

It was a trap. The operator had deliberately been keeping him while they could trace him. While waiting for Oslo to answer, he had momentarily turned his back on the window and in the little mirror at the back of the kiosk he saw their reflection. There were three of them. He turned slowly, his shoulders tense with a sickening fear. The policemen were talking to a little man who was standing by the newspaper stall. He would be the house detective. They were staring in his direction. Fighting down his panic, he replaced the receiver on its rest and went out in the foyer. He didn't look in their direction. A crowd of people were queueing in front of the phone box, and as soon as he went out a woman immediately took his place. He walked purposefully over towards the lifts.

One of the policemen came towards him through the crowd. "Excuse me, Sir," he said quietly. "Routine enquiry, but could you . . ."

Then the little hotel detective was pulling frantically at the policeman's sleeve, and the Minister heard his name mentioned in the whispered explanation that followed.

"So sorry, Minister," the policeman was ruffled now and moved a respectful pace backwards. "Our mistake. Case of mistaken identity. I had no idea . . . I'm investigating a phone call we thought was being made from one of these boxes over there. Only my duty, Sir."

"Not at all Officer. Quite right. What's the trouble?" asked the Minister in a desperate fit of bravado.

"Call to Norway, Sir. Security case. We was checking up on . . ."

"I hope whoever it is had more luck than me. Couldn't get through even to the Chelsea number I was dialling." The Minister smiled, and the policeman laughed back. "Well, goodnight, Officer."

"Goodnight, Sir. Sorry again for troubling you."

The Minister went on over towards the lifts and took one up to the bar on the top floor. He was shaking. He ordered a double whisky and took it neat. The first sip eased things a little and he forced his mind over the events of the past few minutes. The nearness of his capture had almost made him forget something the operator had said—something about the house having been damaged by fire. An odd remark to make in the circumstances, unless it was true. She had been trying to keep him on the line, that was definite enough. But the fire—

yes, it certainly rang true. He shuddered suddenly and swallowed the rest of his whisky at a gulp. He had to get back to the House.

The Duty Officer called Rossetti in, to read the police report. An abortive attempt had been made to get through to Oslo and with luck the police would have caught the caller. But in her excitement, the operator appeared to have got his number wrong, and when the police had traced the one she gave them, which they did in a matter of minutes, it turned out to be a call box at the Hilton. The girl had been so certain, but it just went to show how unreliable the system was. No harm had been done and the Minister of State who had been phoning a Chelsea number from the box had been very nice about it all.

Rossetti picked up his green phone at once and rang MacCaig. "That's enough evidence now, isn't it?" he said plaintively. "You don't need me to go and see him still."

The reply was sharp and to the point.

"Oh God, all right. I'll do it now," said Rossetti, then, remarkably quickly and calmly, he put down the receiver. He waited a moment before picking it up again and getting himself put through to a London number that he only used in emergencies. He let it ring for nearly two minutes but there was no reply.

"Damn, damn, damn," said Rossetti.

TWENTY

Westminster and Mayfair, Thursday Evening

The Minister left the House of Commons five minutes after Rossetti. In the strain of the brief interview, Rossetti's nervousness had appeared only too natural and the Minister was in no frame of mind to notice the elements of deception in the man's story. It came across as a simple attempt at blackmail. Rossetti knew or had guessed. What he wanted in return was, to the Minister, both imprecise and irrelevant.

The Minister had fought down a blind desire to suppress the evidence there and then but he knew it would be madness. He couldn't permanently silence Rossetti on his own. Stefan Issouna would be able to cope. So he bought time: time to find Stefan and time to think. It would be easy. Rossetti had been shaking more than he had. He would be easy to shut up so long as he didn't do anything foolish, tell anyone in the meantime. The Minister had summoned up his reserves of persuasion and believed he had succeeded. He had done it with vast promises without admitting any of the truth. He had told Rossetti nothing that could be used against him later.

The Minister left the House by St. Stephen's Entrance, ignoring the friendly greeting from the policeman on duty. He walked in a daze into Parliament Square and hailed a taxi. As he was swirled away in the evening traffic, he failed to notice the blue Rover 3,500 which pulled out and stayed close behind.

Nicci wasn't there when he arrived at the apartment she used, so he let himself in with a pass key. She had given him it once, encouraged him to use it, but he never had, always slightly apprehensive about what or whom he might find. In the past he had always come by appointment.

He didn't switch on the lights but sat there in the dark in a numb stupor of fear. He thought of trying to reach Stefan again in Oslo, and went so far as to pick up the telephone receiver, but he replaced it at once, realising they would trace him again straight away. He closed his eyes and tried to think.

After what seemed an age, he looked at his watch. In the dark, the fluorescent hands pointed to ten o'clock. He had been sitting there for over an hour. He must move. He must do something. It didn't matter what. To sit like this could only add to his panic. With an effort, he stood up and fumbled his way to the door. Closing it carefully behind him, he went down into the street.

The rain had stopped. Cars were parked tightly nose to tail all along the pavement. At least two of them were occupied. Opposite the door of the block a low black American car was waiting, its engine running softly. A blue Rover 3,500 was parked a few yards further on.

The moment he emerged the Minister heard his name called, and when he turned he recognised Issouna's unmistakable silhouette. The immediate spasm of fear he experienced gave way to a brief new hope, and he smiled back his genuine relief as Issouna held the door open for him.

Hypnotised, he got into the passenger seat and the car at once pulled away from the kerb, along the street and then turned left into the heavy stream of Park Lane traffic.

"What are you doing here and how did you know where I was," he blurted out, as the initial shock wore off. "I have something . . ."

"Relax, Minister. I like to keep track of where you are. It's good news. You should be pleased to see me."

The Minister huddled numbly in the seat. He felt almost secure now after the loneliness of the past few hours. He vaguely took in what Issouna was telling him, that the Norsemen operation had been temporarily called off due to the violence of the opposition to it and because of the Royal Commission, that it was finished and done with for the present.

"And the two who went over to Oslo?" he heard himself asking. "You were kind, weren't you, Stefan? I tried to ring you to say."

"Don't worry about them, Minister. There was an accident. Don't let it rest on your conscience."

"I heard there had been a fire," whispered the Minister, almost to himself. Issouna glanced across quickly at the man in the passenger's seat, who sat there pale and shrunken.

"So why do you worry, Minister? I'll take you home now." Stefan drove the car down past Green Park towards the Mall and Westminster. Once he produced a handkerchief from his pocket and gently caressed his brow. The other hand kept a powerful grip on the steering wheel.

"We could forget, with no harm done to my reputation if only . . ."

"If only what?"

"I've been trying to tell you, Stefan. One of my officials suspects. He came to see me this evening. He was the one you took the briefcase from. He says he came that day at my bidding and thinks I arranged it all, which I didn't. Then he got hold of a transcript of a telephone call I made to you. Your line was bugged."

"I suspected it was," said Issouna quietly. "What is this man's name?"

"He's called Rossetti. A fool, but nonetheless he's trying to blackmail me. Something must be done."

"Something must, something must. What has gone wrong?" The words were hissed rather than spoken and the Minister looked across again, puzzled at the reaction he had produced. At that moment Issouna, who had been driving purposefully down towards Westminster, suddenly swerved in a U-turn across Whitehall and made back up towards Trafalgar Square. He shot the traffic lights as they changed to red and swept left under Admiralty Arch into the Mall. As he went, he glanced constantly in the driving mirror, an unusually tense look on his face. But he appeared reassured by something, and halfway along the Mall he pulled gently into the side of the road under the trees of St. James's Park. Leaving the parking lights on, he switched off the car's engine and turned in his seat towards the Minister. His face, visible only from time to time with the lights from passing cars, was hard and cold.

"You say Rossetti has tried to blackmail you?"

"Yes."

"What does he say he wants?" Issouna spoke sharply.

"I . . . I don't really know. I was so startled, so shaken by him knowing."

"And you didn't ask him?" Issouna was incredulous now.

"Does it matter, Stefan? He wants a bit of patronage, promotion or something. The thing is he knows. *He knows*," the Minister repeated. "What do we do with him, that's the question."

His companion sat in silence for a few seconds before replying. Then, "Leave that to me. I will arrange about Mr. Rossetti," he replied.

"I knew I could rely on you, Stefan." The Minister smiled thankfully. "He won't gossip in the short run, but in the long run . . ."

"In the long run we are all dead, Minister. You should know that. This makes me concerned about the future."

The Minister shivered and glanced across at him, some new warning light glowing in the back of his brain. Stefan had been remarkably upset about the Rossetti revelation, as he himself had been. But now surely it would be all right? As if echoing his thoughts, the face opposite was smiling and relaxed once again. The Minister pathetically followed suit, but his hands still pulled nervously and continuously at the black leather of the car seat.

Behind them in the Mall, a sudden two-tone siren blared, causing the Minister to sit up nervously in his seat. He relaxed again as he recognised the blue flashing lights of a fire engine, and he watched as it went on down towards the Palace and disappeared in the direction of Victoria. A few moments later, with a pretence at confidence, he said: "There's no future to worry about Stefan, we've buried it along with the past. We can forget the Norsemen. Once Rossetti is accounted for, that is."

"The Norsemen, yes; Rossetti, yes. But you and I have a long-term goal, Minister."

Again the warning light glowed, but this time the Minister was prepared. He would play it slowly.

"I don't understand," he said.

"You've been helpful, very helpful. We must continue the struggle."

"It's not on, of course—not on my part. We had a pact. This far and no further, Stefan. Now we tidy up and finish."

The eyes in the hairless head narrowed a fraction, but the smile remained. Issouna stared at the other man. A silk handkerchief was raised slowly to the moist forehead.

"I'm afraid we misunderstood each other, Minister." The voice was low and controlled. "The battlefield has changed, there are some hitches, but the participants remain the same. You surely know me well enough by now."

"I do indeed. But this time it really is all over. I must get the whole Copenhagen history off my chest, and I'm resigning in any case; you may have heard. Your hold is going to be broken, Stefan, though I hold you no ill-will. You're just doing your job. I appreciate that."

As he spoke, the Minister had been nervously fiddling with a row of control buttons on the black panelling of the dashboard in front of him. He accidentally pressed one on the radio and immediately the car was filled with the raucous, irrelevant music of a pop station. He hurriedly switched off again.

Issouna frowned at the interruption. "I am glad to be appreciated, Minister. Yes, I had heard you were thinking of resigning. But to employ the words you used a moment ago—it's not on, of course."

"You obviously don't understand, Stefan. I must make a completely clean break with my past. I am going to make an appointment with the Prime Minister tomorrow morning. He may criticise but he certainly won't want a fuss and will realise from the little I tell him about my past in Copenhagen, that it happened a long time ago. And about our more recent . . . er . . . contacts, there'll be no proof, after Rossetti, that is."

"After Rossetti, precisely. But you want my help there." Issouna dabbed with the handkerchief at his face and lips as he spoke. The Minister emulated the man and removed incipient sweat from his own face with the back of his hand.

"So you see, you will have to help in turn. You will not speak to your Prime Minister, and you will help." The tone was sharper now and menacing. "You are of great use to us, but only in your present position of influence. You will help because the alternative is for us to let Rossetti tell people how co-operative you have been."

"You're not threatening me?" In a dream the Minister reacted with amazement, tried to smile, tried to indicate how ridiculous it all seemed. He suddenly felt starved of air and wound the car window right down.

"How melodramatic the British always are. You call my explanation a threat? But I think you know what I mean. We give you three or four weeks' grace and we will be in touch again. You will not do anything foolish as the effects would be politically and personally disastrous for you. Now I have work to do if you want the Rossetti problem out of the way. And I am late in returning to Oslo, where I have one or two ends to tie up. They expected me back yesterday. If you will forgive me."

Issouna returned his handkerchief to his pocket, looked at his watch and slowly switched on the ignition. As he did so he glanced automatically in the rear mirror. Something he saw there made him frown momentarily. He put the car into gear let out the clutch and moved forward into the Mall traffic. The Minister stayed slouched in the passenger seat. After a few hundred yards and just short of Buckingham Palace, Issouna suddenly pulled into the side once again. The Minister looked across at him enquiringly as the blue Rover shot past and came to a halt about fifty yards further on.

"As I thought," said Stefan Issouna quietly. "You are not only weak but a fool as well."

The Minister blinked without comprehension. "What is it, Stefan?"

"You, *we*, are being followed."

"Followed? I don't see."

Issouna indicated the blue Rover. "I had suspected something earlier, but even I was convinced it was nothing."

"Are you sure?" the Minister burst out.

Stefan nodded slowly.

"Then it's Rossetti. Damn, I thought . . ."

"No, it's not Rossetti, it couldn't be, unless . . ."

"I don't understand, Stefan."

"Nor do I, for the moment." The answer came without haste or panic.

"What do we do, Stefan? What do we do?" Realisation was dawning slowly on him and he crumpled up, terror etched across his face. The normally handsome features had vanished in the creases of his anxiety. "What do we do? What do we do? You must help me, Stefan." The Minister's words stumbled forth, repeating themselves and rising to near scream. He was leaning across now and gripping the other man's jacket.

Issouna pushed him off roughly. "What do *you* do, you mean. I am going to open this door, get out and walk away. You may do as you can or as you choose."

"Stefan, you can't leave me. Stefan. You wouldn't. No, Stefan. No." The Minister was whimpering now. The other man looked across at the huddled figure with contempt.

"I can and I will. Goodbye, Minister."

"But you'll be stopped. You're in this with me. You'll be arrested. Yes, you've had it too. We're in it together," the Minister gabbled.

"They may well stop me, but as I have taken the precaution of providing myself with diplomatic status and a diplomatic passport, there is little they can do. I have done nothing legally wrong, though your Government may declare me *persona non grata* and expel me. You are rather different," he shrugged.

The Minister sat pale and silent, gazing at him with horror as the full enormity of his position was brought home. He glanced fearfully at the blue Rover which he could still make out, parked a little way in front. Then Issouna was reaching for the door handle, opening it and stepping out into the night. Slamming the car door behind him he bent down and spoke through the open window:

"You may like to have this," he said softly. Something hard and metallic landed on the black leather of the driver's seat. "It's loaded. It would be for the best . . . if you have the courage."

The Minister grasped wildly at the gun and, picking it up, stared at it as if hypnotised. Perhaps it was the way and Stefan was right. It could solve everything. He brought it up level with his face. Staring at the small black mouth of the barrel, he pointed it straight at himself. He shut his eyes and began to apply pressure to the trigger.

Then the moment of truth welled up inside him. For what seemed an interminable age the end was inevitable, irrefutable. And then, through the despair, a shaft of lucidity showed that there was another conceivable way of shedding the albatross.

Something snapped in the back of the Minister's brain. Quickly he opened the door and stepped from the car. He stood for a moment and watched Issouna as he began to walk away along the Mall.

Then, "Stefan," he called in a still small voice. "Stefan."

Stefan Issouna turned enquiringly, his bald head glistening in the lamplight. As he did so, the Minister brought up the gun and shot him through the heart.

Perhaps the noise of the traffic deadened the sound, for the people in the blue Rover did not move. The scene had also been partly obscured by Issouna's car, and the body now lay askew and oddly crumpled on the tarmac at its rear.

The Minister, curiously cold and self-possessed, paused momentarily, then strode slowly and purposefully towards the Rover. As he approached, people started scrambling out of all four doors. MacCaig, Tesco, the girl, and two plain-clothes men. The Minister ignored the others and went up to MacCaig.

"I'm glad you're here," he said quickly. "The man you are

looking for is over there. I have just shot him. I think he's dead. He pulled a gun, we struggled and there was no alternative." He spoke with no visible sign of emotion. The immensity of his action had deadened every nerve in him.

For some moments the five stared uncomprehendingly back at the Minister who stood facing them, pale almost distinguished and composed by the roadside. The lights from the passing cars alternately lit up his face and plunged it into darkness. Then, at a signal from MacCaig, the two plain-clothes men ran forward towards the other car and the body at its rear.

"Will you take me to a police station. I will have to make a statement." It was an order rather than a request. "I must also make some telephone calls urgently. There will be a manslaughter case I expect, and I should warn the Prime Minister of the possibility. Leave your men to cope here. And hurry please."

The Minister's composure and authority were complete. The drawn look in his face had set into a hardness that might only be understandable in the circumstances. Heightened by the drama of the situation, a bewildering, all-questioning doubt had gripped the others and there was no alternative but to comply.

TWENTY-ONE

Westminster, Thursday Night

On an Albert Embankment bench, below the uninspiring towers of the new St. Thomas's Hospital, a young couple were huddled in excited private debate, despite the torrential rain. The river below seemed as deceptively sluiced and freshened by the downpour as the two black-tarred Port of London Authority barges which lay at their mid-stream anchor. In the background, the constant roar of London by night had been toned down to the gentler swish of countless tyres on the wet tarmac.

Across the river, the light in the little mock-Gothic tower above Big Ben told those who wanted to know that the House was still sitting. It was close on quarter to twelve, but the evening papers had warned of the likelihood of an all-night debate on the new tax legislation. A Three-Line Whip had been issued.

The blue Rover turned through the heavy wrought-iron gates and cleaved its way across the pools of water on the courtyard, to the main door of the House. The policeman inside saluted the Minister but tried to stop the others. MacCaig and the two Special Branch men were about to produce their passes when the Minister waved them through. "They're with me," he said to the officer. "They're coming to make sure I vote," he added with a smile.

That was almost true. Someone on a charge of manslaughter couldn't be allowed off on his own just because he was a Minister of the Crown who had to vote as required by the Three-Line Whip. It had been necessary for the Prime Minister, to whom the vote that night was more immediately crucial than some squalid scandal involving one of his junior Ministers, to speak to the Police Commissioner himself. Such things could wait till the morning, and tonight the rules had been just a fraction bent.

The Minister was extremely elated. He had told the partial truth. They believed it was the whole truth. If they had some lingering doubts, then it was too bad. They could prove nothing now that Stefan was dead. He could relax. Certainly there was the remaining unpleasantness of the manslaughter charge. Certainly people would think he had had some peculiar link with the dead man, but it was a welcome alternative to what a few hours ago had seemed inevitable. Even the threat from Rossetti now seemed absurd and remote. He could think more clearly now, and what did that amount to? A couple of monitored phone calls to the dead man. What was wrong with that? He wasn't going to deny that he knew Stefan well and that Stefan had tried to blackmail him with his friendship. He had done the right thing and laughed in Stefan's face, said he was going to the police. That was when Stefan had pulled a gun on him. As he had repeated earlier, there was no alternative. Stefan had meant to kill him. Nor was there a worry about Rossetti. Quite the opposite. He had simply been another blackmailer and there would have to be a follow-up on him as well. There was only that odd accusation, which both Stefan and Rossetti made, about him ringing Rossetti and getting him to bring the files. But that was nonsense. While he had never done that, it left a question mark.

But there was every reason for the Minister's elation. And the manslaughter trial? Well, he was going to resign in any case. He would make sure that the real story, as he would have it known, would be well publicised. A vindication as the main article on the front of one of the quality Sundays? Or maybe that was a bit vulgar. "The Minister who saved the Nation from the forces of evil, from the Norsemen."

The Minister led the other men through the corridors to the Central Lobby.

"I have to go into the Chamber now, it's nearly time for the vote. The Opposition spokesman has just finished." The

Minister glanced up at one of the closed-circuit television screens which relayed the proceedings throughout the Palace of Westminster.

"That's all right, Minister. We'll just follow," said MacCaig politely.

"You obviously don't know the workings of the House of Commons, MacCaig," replied the Minister loftily. "You can't come with me. Only Members are allowed through into the Chamber and on to the floor of the House."

"But this is an exception. We have instructions."

"I can assure you, the House of Commons is one of the last refuges of scoundrels. I can't be arrested here. You would be breaching my privilege, to use the accepted expression. But don't worry, MacCaig, I'm not going to abscond. As you know, I have done nothing to be ashamed of."

MacCaig and the two Special Branch men reluctantly allowed themselves to be separated from their ward. As the Minister left them to go on to the floor of the House, he spoke to one of the House messengers and told him to take the three men up to the Strangers' Gallery. They could watch the remainder of the debate from there. "You can keep an eye on me as well, if it will make you happier. We'll meet again later." The Minister turned away laughing and greeted a colleague cheerfully as he went along the hall towards the debate.

Cannon Row Police Station, Thursday Night

The police officer showed them into a bare, green painted room. He gave them pens and paper, and left. Fiona Ross and Walt Tesco had been left there at the police station and were about to try writing their statements while still in a thoroughly confused state of mind.

"It proves that we jumped to conclusions too quickly, over the Minister I mean. He's had a hard time, that man. I'm glad it's all nearly over. It's been like a bad dream." Fiona sat nursing her head in her hands.

"Yes," said Tesco slowly. "But there are one or two ends

that don't quite tie up. What Rossetti said can't be all meaningless. And someone told Issouna about your coming to Oslo. There's the record of that telephone conversation. It's all circumstantial I admit, but it does point pretty convincingly at one man."

"Well, there's no proof, so that's that."

"And why is there no proof? Because Stefan Issouna is dead, perhaps?"

"No, I can't believe it. The Minister isn't that sort of man. He couldn't have done it in cold blood."

"Well, we'll leave it for the moment. Perhaps by the trial things will look different."

"I don't expect so. This has got a lot of political dynamite packed inside it. It will be in everyone's interests to keep the temperature down. Whatever happens we'll get a cover-up operation even if there turns out to be something fantastic to hide. The Minister will emerge with a conditional release as if he had only killed a man by accident when driving."

The door of the little room opened and a police officer came in.

"You Mr. Tesco?" he asked.

"Yes, that's me. Why?"

"Well, we've just been going through the dead man's pockets, Mr. Tesco. There was a sealed letter to you inside the wallet. We've been making a list of his belongings you understand. It's normal practice."

"A letter to me?" said Tesco stupidly.

"That's what I said. Inspector asks if you could kindly step along and open it in his presence."

In the Inspector's office, Tesco nervously slit the envelope open, took out the unsigned memorandum and began to read. It referred to the previous promise of revelations which these now were. There was a lot in it about the Minister. Stefan Issouna had been carrying it as an insurance, to threaten the Minister if his other blandishments had failed.

Tesco stood up. As he did so he noticed white powder on his hands. The police had been checking for fingerprints.

Westminster, Thursday Night and Friday Morning

The Chancellor of the Exchequer was winding up a long and tedious debate for the Government. He was matching the occasion with an uninspired and halting speech, and most of the M.P.s, who were only there because of the Three-Line Whip in any case, seemed half asleep. It was now a quarter past midnight. The only signs of attentiveness on the faces of the listeners were associated with a constant watch to see when the man was going to come to the end of his remarks and the Speaker would be able to put the question. Spectators watching from the Stranger's Gallery realised, like so many visitors had done in the past, how boring and dull the parliamentary life of a Member of the House of Commons could be.

There was a perceptible stir both on the floor and in the Galleries when the Minister came into the Chamber. He pushed himself casually into the already overcrowded Government Front Bench and lolled back on the green leather as if he, for one, had not a care in the world. He went so far as to emulate some of the more senior colleagues and put his feet up on the Clerk's Table that separated the two sides of the House of Commons. He looked every inch a man at peace.

Inside himself, however, he was curious at the stir that had greeted his entry. They must know already that he had been involved in this shooting incident. Perhaps the P.M. himself, sitting in his allotted place at the end of the Treasury Bench, had passed the word on. Then the Minister noticed an early edition of one of the national dailies which was lying with some more official papers in the lap of one of his colleagues. He leant forward and took hold of the newspaper mouthing a smile and a wordless "May I?" to the man who had it. The paper already had the gist of the story. Like so many, perhaps its crime writers listened in to the police networks in the evenings to get early warning of a story. He saw his own name. It didn't say that he had done the shooting, and it called Stefan a nameless "diplomat", but it did manage to fit the "Norsemen" into the copy. For the benefit of the many watching him, he shook his head sadly as he read, and then handed it back with a wry smile and a shrug, as if to say, "Well, you know how papers sensationalise things".

He lolled back in his seat again, watching the Chancellor of the Exchequer without taking in any of his words. With this latest fuss, and now he was thinking of it as a mere fuss, the top jobs like the Chancellorship would be closed to him in politics. But he wasn't sorry and there were other fields in which a wisp of notoriety, which this case would bring him, would stand him in good stead. No, he wasn't worried.

Then a drink-smelling voice was whispering something incoherent in his ear. On the bench behind, the Right Honourable Fergus Smith, former Junior Minister, former promising young politician, the present-day totally alcoholic back-bencher, was leaning forward telling him something. The Minister hardly listened, smiled kindly and nodded his head. Poor old Fergus Smith, a broken reed of a man, someone who once had been well-known and could have risen to the very top if excess time spent in the bars of the House and everywhere else hadn't stunted his prowess. Late at night like this, Fergus Smith was often to be seen trying to trap some more senior man and would pour forth some hiccoughed, burping story of little or no importance.

The Minister turned his head slightly to avoid the worst of the stench of stale alcohol. But then something the old man was whispering struck home. He turned in his seat and looked at him.

"What was that again, Fergus," he asked quietly.

". . . outside, waiting for you. The Clerk of the House has spoken to the Speaker, but he says they'll have to wait. It would breach the sanctity of the House," he slurred, ". . . to let them arrest you here. A breach of privilege."

"Oh you mean my escort. They're waiting for me up there in the Strangers' Gallery. They're all right," the Minister whispered back with a smile, looking up, as he did so, to where he knew MacCaig was sitting with the two plain-clothes men.

At once he saw that something new had happened. Fiona

Ross and the journalist were there with the Police Inspector who was in charge of security at the Palace of Westminster. They were whispering, pointing down at him. A tail-coated messenger, his silver chain of office dangling angrily from his neck, was trying to silence them. No talking was allowed in the Strangers' Gallery.

"That lot up there had a job getting into the House at all," Fergus Smith continued to breathe rapidly in his ear. "They've found a letter on the diplomat's body or something. It's all about you. They were talking to the Clerk and I overheard them saying something about arresting you as soon as you leave the House. I thought if you're in trouble of some sort I'd better warn you. You've always been kind enough to me."

Fergus Smith paused momentarily for breath, then he spoke more urgently: ". . . Hey, wait a minute Minister, where are you going? You can't leave now. The Speaker's just about to divide the House, and there's a Three-Line Whip, remember."

When one stares directly at the sun or at a light bulb and then shuts one's eyes, an image is left on the retina for a considerable period of time. Though some hours had elapsed, as the Minister strode quickly out of the startled Chamber, all he could see was an image of the slightly glistening bald head as Issouna had fallen that last time. Stefan Issouna had won in the end, and this was the end for him as well. It might at least lead to real peace of mind.

He went from the Chamber by a side entrance, only partly aware, as he left, of every eye being on him, of the extra hesitation in the Chancellor of the Exchequer's voice, of the struggling in the Strangers' Gallery where MacCaig and the others were trying to get past the duty-conscious attendants and follow him.

Through the complex, panelled side-corridors of the Palace of Westminster; up by an oak stairway hung with many portraits of famous parliamentarians; past an inconspicuous little alcove by the top where he failed to notice the elegant, drawn figure of Rossetti standing waiting for him; at last to the transient sanctuary of his own room. He would wait for them there, poised and ready in his own chosen environment. The fear, the terror, had gone and he was prepared.

In international espionage, for every one spy or traitor dramatically uncovered, a hundred remain hidden. Otherwise, who would be a spy? The ones who are unearthed, the tip of the iceberg, are those who have been caught out by being too flamboyant, too careless or who have attempted things beyond their capability and the opaqueness of their cover.

So the grey men hundreds of miles to the east, who had also employed the late Stefan Issouna, had known too well what they were doing when they had recruited Rossetti. At the Oxford of the late 'forties he was, in every external action as in his appearance, a well-bred, effete, gossiping bore; a man to be laughed at, despised or even disliked; a man never remotely suspected of being capable of deep deceit; an arch-type buffoon to be avoided or, at least, ignored.

Because of all these things, because of this most effective of natural disguises, they had eagerly recruited Rossetti. He, in turn, had been a willing volunteer to a calling which gave him, in the end, a real and hidden superiority over those who mocked him. He had taken care to impress people in the Ministry only sufficiently for them to continue to employ him. As an agent it was different. He was called on only in the most infrequent and most important occasions and those who twitched the strings controlling him knew, as Rossetti himself knew, that, as a result, he would remain hidden and unsuspected.

And so it was. On instructions, Rossetti had played his part, had even manipulated his own beating up and for the files to be stolen in a way that he would later be able to use to further compromise the Minister. He had arranged to get the telephone call which he could pretend to his colleagues was a ministerial summons. But in fact it had been the other way about. On his way out with the files he had stopped and made a call from Reception, not about being possibly late for his dinner appointment as he had claimed, but to the Minister's Private Office to say he was coming across to brief the Minister on the Norsemen. He was thus expected, but not summoned by the Minister. Rossetti the expert knew the workings of Whitehall well, and rightly judged that in a busy Private Office no one would check the sequence of events. Only the Minister might be puzzled later, but Rossetti and, in his turn, Stefan Issouna, could judge their timing in inserting into a confused and tired mind the accusation that the Minister had manipulated the whole thing from the outset. When the memory of the Copenhagen affair had perhaps lost some of its terror and hold over the Minister, there would be such fall-back methods of tying him to his unchosen role. But Rossetti had to pursue his overt role as well, often not too difficult a task, as when he had on behalf of his Ministry, baited Tesco with details of the Norsemen and then later had been forced to start casting doubt on the Minister, again putting on an elaborate act with Tesco, to cover up his own involvement in the stolen files. By that stage it had suited both sets of players.

Yet it had gone too far. A professional hazard in all character assassination exercises is to avoid straining the victim to the limits of his obedience. Here it had happened. Two rules of this game of compromising had been broken; the victim had both bitten back and had been over exposed. He had made an error of judgement over Tesco, never believing he would go on a successful rescue mission to Oslo on his own. That had been careless and avoidable. Not so the impulse which had driven the Minister to shoot Stefan, and the unplanned discovery of the letter which had only been constructed as a means of applying further pressure on the Minister; but together these all meant that as an agent the Minister was now valueless. More than that, he was dangerous, for if he now were to confess to everything he had done, every way he had helped, then many still valuable links, people and plans might become exposed. The death of Stefan was also something that had to be atoned for. So the order had come: to revenge and to silence, but mainly to silence.

Rossetti came silently into the room where the Minister stood frozen in his own limbo. He was up beside him before the other man noticed. Balanced professionally in a gloved hand, the little gun was brought up to the Minister's temple and one shot was fired. Rossetti stood back with distaste as the body collapsed in a heap on the carpet. He bent down quickly and pressed the Minister's fingers tightly once or twice round the butt, then let the gun drop away from the lifeless fingers.

He stood up and walked rapidly towards the door. There was little time, but he paused momentarily and looked back, reverting to type as he did so.

"How untidy of me. How very untidy. A beautiful carpet ruined," Rossetti breathed quietly to himself. Then he ran blindly from the room, out into the corridor, past the group of grim-faced men advancing on the Minister's door. As he went he was shouting about a suicide, a revolver and the great red stain spreading slowly across the carpet's intricate Persian design.